STUFF THAT

Adam Millard is the author of twenty-nine novels, seventeen novellas, and more than two hundred short stories, which can be found in various collections and anthologies. Probably best known for his post-apocalyptic fiction, Adam also writes fantasy/horror for children, as well as bizarro fiction for several publishers. His work has been translated for the German, Spanish, and Russian Markets. Adam lives in Newcastle-under-Lyme with his wife, Dawn, and their two cats, Butter and Toast.

STUFF THAT

ADAM MILLARD

A CIP catalogue record for this book
is available from the British Library

ISBN: 978-1-7384764-7-3

Crowded Quarantine Publications
124 Dimsdale Parade West
Newcastle-under-Lyme
Staffordshire
ST5 8DU

"But when I make a good [taxidermy] mount I feel like I beat God in a small way. As though the Almighty said, Let such critter be dead, and I said, 'Fuck You, he can still play the banjo.'"

- Christopher Buehlman

1

The woman approached the counter, carrier bag dangling from her emaciated wrist on one side and a small child dangling from the other. The child's feet were barely touching the floor, which might have had something to do with the fact it was upside-down, for the woman fairly carried that kid the way one might carry a refuse sack or drunken midget. The child knew better than to complain, though, even when its upside-down face clonked against a leg of the proprietor's workbench.

Ted Barker stopped what he was doing—*The Sun*'s prize-winning Su-Doku—and gave the woman his full attention. He immediately wished he hadn't, for she looked like something which had passed through the interior workings of a hungry lion. Her eyes were too far apart, for one, giving her the appearance of a reptile, and her aquiline nose extended down almost to her chin. In other words, Ted didn't fancy her at all. "Can I help you?" He leaned across the counter and glanced down at the child dangling from the woman's left hand. He sighed. "You do realise," he said, "that this is a taxidermist's, and not an orphanage?"

The woman cursed—and a terrible curse word it was, too—and flipped the child over so that it was the right way up.

Ted recoiled in horror; there was no mistaking the child belonged to the woman. It had the same eyes, the same nose, poor little bastard.

"You'll have to excuse Marnie," said the woman, motioning to the unfortunate pile of limbs and flesh comprising her daughter. "She's got this thing, you see, where her features are all jumbled up. Looks a right bloody mess, don't it?" She poked at Marnie's face. Marnie simply went on drooling.

"Er, yes," Ted said, for what *else* could he say? "I wonder where she gets it from?" Apparently he could say *that*. Turning his attention to the woman—lest the sight of Marnie get the better of his gag-reflex—Ted nodded at the carrier bag. "I take it you have an animal for me. Was it a pet? Are you selling a cadaver? Is it something you and your daughter just jumped out on, thusly terrifying it to death in an instant?"

The woman shook her head. "Cat," she said, slamming it down on the counter. "Misty, female tortoiseshell. Don't want her back, just selling her on, you know."

"And am I right in understanding that this cat, Misty, was a friend of your daughter's?" He looked sadly upon the little girl across the counter, heaved twice, and said, "No, I tried, but is there any chance you could ask Marnie to wait outside. I had a lovely mushroom omelette for breakfast, and it would be a terrible shame to see it perform an encore."

"Marnie, go and wait outside," said the woman, waving the girl away dismissively. Once she was gone—and the little fucker kicked Gerry the baby giraffe in the shins as she went—the woman began to peel the plastic bag from the dead animal. "She's a lovely specimen, if I do say so myself."

"And you do, do you?"

"I do what?"

"Say so yourself?"

"That I do, my friend," said the woman. "You ain't ever seen a dead cat like this one, I can guarantee it."

Ted was intrigued, which was strange, really, since dead cats seldom intrigued him. They were ten-a-penny, thanks to the ring road. Now, bring him a dead chimp and he *would* be impressed, and not just because chimps are usually very good at crossing duel carriageways. Exotic animals were his favourites. Cats were not exotic; you could dress a tabby in a Hawaiian tee-shirt and drape a lei around its neck and it would still look shit. No, Ted had a whole box of dead cats in the freezer out back. He didn't know whether he would ever get around to stuffing them, or if he'd end up selling them, as he had done on one or two occasions before, to *Ho Chi Minh's Dragon Lounge Buffet and Bar*—eat as much as you like, but don't take the piss.

"Mom, there's a man out here offering me sweets if I get in the car with him," Marnie said as she reappeared in the doorway.

"Ask him what kind of sweets," said the woman as

she continued to fiddle with the carrier bag.

Ted was shocked, and appalled, and shocked yet again as the ugly little sprout proceeded to ask the man idling at the kerb the nature of his suck. After a few seconds she shouted—and dribbled a little—into the shop. "Says he's got blackjacks."

The woman shook her head. "You don't like blackjacks, Marnie. They make your mouth all dark, remember."

"Oh, yeah," Marnie said. She called outside. "I don't like blackjacks. They make my mouth all dark." Then came the sound of a car making off at speed, and Marnie returned to the outside world, where she would be fortunate to ever receive such a generous offer again.

"Is this going to take long," Ted said, watching the woman working away at a double-knot. "I've got a parrot to do for a client this afternoon, and it's a tricky one." Parrots were not usually tricky, but the customer—a little old dear by the name of Martha Tickle—wanted Derrick (not all parrots are called Polly, you know) to be part of a nice scene, with deckchairs, and beach huts, and sandcastles. And Ted had never attempted to stuff a sandcastle before, so he wasn't particularly looking forward to it.

"Hang on," said the woman. "There, got it!" She upended the carrier bag and out onto the counter fell a dead cat. "See!" she said. "Told you you ain't never seen a dead cat like our Misty."

Ted nodded. "You are correct, madam," he said,

"because that cat is very much alive."

"Don't be ridiculous!" gasped the woman. "That is the deadest cat I have ever seen in my life!"

Meow, said Misty.

"It just said 'Meow'," Ted said. "Dead cats don't meow."

"Yes they bloody well do!" The woman was exasperated, and also completely mental. "I saw a programme once which said that a gassy build-up can manifest after death by way of the vocal cords—"

"I am fully *aware* of what is possible following death," Ted said, "but your cat is now urinating all over my Su-Doku."

"I know. Sad, isn't it? Poor Misty, taken too soon."

"Are you on medication, lady?" Ted was fairly losing his rag now, and not just because his chance of winning £100 cash plus free entry into a Bognor Regis camping holiday prize-pot had gone for a Burton. "I can't take your cat on account that it is not dead. It still breathes. It's very much alive and well, apart from possible brain-damage from being double-knotted into a plastic carrier-bag."

"Well, if *you* won't take it," the woman said, scooping Misty up into her skeletal and liveried arms, "then I'll have no other choice but to sell it to *Ho Chi Minh's Dragon Lounge Buffet and Bar.*"

"There is a cattery not three miles from this very building," Ted said.

"*Ho*'s is closer," replied the woman, and with that she

turned and marched for the door, leaving her shit- and piss-filled carrier bag on the counter. She yanked the door open and yelled, "Marnie… what have I told you about playing in the road? Look out! Ah, fuck it! Marnie? Marnie, bloody hell, you're all squashed!" She turned to Ted, who was trying to dry his puzzle out by rubbing the pages upon his person. "I don't suppose you buy the cadavers of flattened children, do you?"

"I suggest you call an ambulance," Ted said.

"Just *what* is the point of your shop?" said the woman, seemingly disgusted, and then she was gone, screaming at the top of her voice—No, *she's not a Chupacabra, you cheeky bastard, she's my daughter! Stop taking pictures!* —and the door slammed shut.

It would be an hour before Ted heard sirens out in the street, which just goes to show that the uglier your child, the less fuss the emergency services make about getting to them in a good and reasonable time.

2

Ted Barker hadn't always been a taxidermist. His father was a taxidermist, and his father before him, and so on and so forth all the way back to the advent of dead animals. There was a rumour—one which Ted was loath to believe—that the first taxidermist Barker had a cave filled with stuffed velociraptors and pterodactyls. This, of course, was ridiculous. Caves simply weren't that big.

Ted Barker had never set out to follow in the footsteps of his father, to continue the family trade. As a child the sight of a dead fly had knocked him bandy. At the age of seven he had stumbled somewhat fortuitously across a mangled badger at the side of the road and had spent the following three days in a catatonic state, only broken by endless hours of vomiting.

Death, it seemed, was everywhere.

Growing up, Ted had studied hard and spent as little time as possible in his father's workshop, which was cluttered with the corpses of various perished fauna, myriad broken-limbed beasties, and a plethora of pancaked rodents. His father, Malcolm Barker, persisted, hoping that, one day, Ted would have a change of heart, or at least grow used to the sight of a cabbaged squirrel. *Take a look at this cabbaged squirrel,* he would say, thrusting the thing under Ted's nose, and Ted would upchuck just as violently as always, and his father would march back to his workshop, muttering disappointedly under his breath.

Finishing school with decent grades, and unsurprisingly with his virginity still intact, Ted had signed up to the nearest college—Snow Hill—intent on learning as much as he could about the works of Shakespeare, Dostoyevsky, and Dickens, but, as with all plans, things quickly turned to shit. An argument in Literature class one day—why do you think Lovecraft was so damn miserable all the damn time? —had turned into a free-for-all. Three teachers had been suspended, along with fifteen students, and the resulting fire scorched the college to its foundations.

Such was the power of HP Lovecraft.

Ted had been banished from the campus and ordered never to return, and why would he? There wasn't much appeal to sitting atop a pile of blackened rubble, not unless you were HP Lovecraft.

"I told you English was for nonces," his father had said upon Ted's return to the family home. "Best thing that could have happened to you, in my opinion. You'd have ended up like that Oscar Wilde fella."

"What?" Ted had asked. "Hugely successful in my field?"

"In jail for gross indecency toward men," his father had so delicately put it. "No, your place is here. Oh, and your grandfather died while you were gone, so there's an opening in the workshop."

"Grandfather's dead?"

"Look, do you want the bloody job or not?" His father had had his hand up a stoat at the time, and Ted wasn't sure that declining the offer of steady pay was in the stoat's best interest.

Ted had nothing. There was no English course at the college because the college was nothing more than cinders, and there was no money in Ted's back pocket because the college fire had burned a hole right through it. With no prospects, and no money, Ted had had no choice but to accept his father's proposition, to learn how to stuff animals, how to make them look real whilst dressing them in miniature clothes and taping various musical instruments and golf-clubs to their limbs, how to give their distraught owners a small amount of happiness—because how sad could you stay if you were faced with an entire scene in which your pet rabbit sat behind a cell door wearing striped clothes while a trio of rats, adorned in all the accoutrements of a modern-day police officer, went about the tedium of their day at the station? I dare you not to laugh.

"For your first anthropomorphic piece," his father had told him on his inaugural day, "you're going to be making this duck look like he's enjoying a picnic of jam sandwiches and Victoria sponge cake whilst also appearing very aware of a nearby hornet's nest."

"That's incredibly specific," Ted had opined.

"The first rule of Taxidermy Club," said his father, "is that we don't question what our clients ask for. We simply do. I once dressed a chinchilla as Adolf Hitler. Did I wonder why my client wanted a racist rodent on their bedside cabinet? Of course I bloody well did! That's fucking ridiculous! But did I voice my concern, ask them to reconsider for something more appropriate; a Martin Luthor King Cobra, perhaps, or a Ratma Gandhi? No, because the customer is always right, even when they're being absurd."

Ted had nodded along, all the time staring down at the thawed-out duck and swallowing saliva by the bucket-load. He would not be sick… he would not be sick… he would not be sick…

"Are you going to be sick?" His father was not a fool.

"If I did," Ted had said, "would you think any less of me?"

"Certainly." He'd picked the duck up and flipped it over. "But no one is ever truly proud of their children. Now, shall we…?"

That afternoon had been one of the most terrifying of Ted's life. The skinning! The peeling! The tanning! All great titles for 1970s horror films, but not a terribly nice way to spend a Sunday afternoon. Ted had watched in horror as his father went about turning that dead sonofabitch into a work of Anatidae Art. He'd insisted upon Ted's participation, and Ted had assisted as much as possible without becoming an actual accomplice. And, despite his initial nausea and apprehension, something happened during the course of that afternoon, something changed. Ted began to enjoy the work, the removal of the skin, the cleaning and the fingering, the degreasing, the pretending-to-make-the-duck-talk-like-a-wooden-dummy—

"Can you not do that?" his father had said, snatching the duck from Ted's hands. "Make yourself useful, son, and pass me that polyurethane foam mannequin."

It would, his father had told him, be a few days before they'd be able to finish the duck, but when they did, and that duck stood there with a jam sandwich in one hand and a wasp-swatter in the other, Ted was sold.

This was what he wanted to do.

This was his destiny.

His calling.

And that, as they say, was that.

3

Ted moved around BARKER'S STUFFED EMPORIUM (est. 1901 – We stuff things so you can stare at them forever!) and, as he so often did during quiet periods, talked to his mounted creatures. For some, this would be considered crazy. *"He talks to them, you know?"* people said. *"I bet that's not all he does to them,"* the more deviant people suggested. Ted didn't give a stuff what people said behind his back; some of his best conversations had been had with a decapitated bear's head.

"Jemima/Jessica!" he said, stroking the hardened feathers of his most controversial piece, a two-headed duck he'd created over a decade ago. "How are you this morning? What's that? You're fed up with one another's company? Oh, come now, there's no need to be like that, Jessica. She is not a cunt… yes, I completely understand that it's not much of an afterlife, but if you could just get along… Now, Jemima, you will not shit on Jessica's foot. For one, it's not nice, and secondly, it's not biologically possible. Excuse me? You'll just fart dust at her then? Now, behave yourself. I really wish we didn't have to have this conversation every single morning… no, Jemima, I will not just fuck off over there with the rat on a unicycle. Show some respect to your creator… That's more like it. Now, I'm going to leave you two alone for a moment while I have a word with Hooter… Yes, I know he's a casual racist, but he's an owl, for fuck's sake. What do you want me to do? No, I can't just 'put him in the bin', that's a terrible thing to say… Look, I've got to go. I can hear Vladimir squeaking at me in Russian, and you know what he gets like if I don't polish that unicycle of his."

Ted left the quarrelsome two-headed duck to its own devices—which weren't much, to be honest—and crossed the room to where Hooter perched upon a thick branch inside a huge glazed case. "And how are you, this morning, Hooter? Yes, it is a new shirt, thanks for asking. I got it at Debenhams last week. Yes, Hooter, I do believe that Polish man still works there… HOOTER! Take it down a few notches, yeah?" Ted checked across his shoulder, made sure no one was within earshot of the casually-racist barn owl. He knew he was the only one who could hear the stuffed animals, that he was merely imagining them as sentient beings, and not the overpriced ornaments they now were, but playfully pretending that they were really speaking to him made it all the more fun, and racism was not acceptable, imagined or otherwise. "So, what do you have planned for today, Hooter? Oh, you might just stand there, huh? You might just stand there on your branch looking toward the door? You might just stand there watching the world go by outside, the young, the old, the illegal immigrants—HOOTER! Seriously, we're going to have to have a little talk about this. You do know you're upsetting the two-headed duck with this nonsense… Yes, Jemima and Jessica told me that they can't bear your xenophobic outbursts… I will not tell them to shove it up their shared arsehole… Hooter, just be aware that your thoughts and beliefs can be hurtful at times, okay? And please, if we do have customers of colour in today, try to control yourself. I'm tired of making excuses for you."

Before the owl could respond—or not, as reality would have it—Ted paced across to where Vladimir balanced perpetually upon his vintage unicycle. He pulled a miniature chamois from his back pocket and proceeded to polish the Russian rodent's wheel. "And how is everyone's favourite ratty circus act on this fine morning? Yes, I appreciate your wheel isn't going to polish itself, Vladimir, but there are a hundred things I need to do in order to keep the shop up to a certain standard, and… No, the 'bastard' owl did not have anything to say about you. You do realise Russia is not a race, don't you? Well, yes he might be prejudiced toward rodents, but I think that has more to do with the fact you're his natural prey… No, I'm not making excuses for him, Vladimir, it's just that if he looks at you funny during the day, it's most likely because he's wondering what you taste like and not because he's picturing you digging your own grave in some Nazi concentration camp. Now, if you'll let me finish polishing your unicycle in peace… No, I haven't had a chance to ask Buffalo Bill about the fiver you lent him last week, but I'm sure you'll get it back." He stopped polishing for a moment and regarded the buffalo head hanging upon the wall to his right. "Bill! Sorry, mate, I didn't mean to wake you, but Vladimir here was wondering when he should expect his money back?" A pause as the buffalo head drowsily responded—or not, as reality would have it. To Vladimir, Ted recounted what the buffalo head had told him. "He says he's put it on a dead-cert at Aintree, and that you'll get it back when he collects his winnings on Thursday." It was the rodent's turn to speak; Ted grimaced as the long string of profanities poured from the rodent's tiny face. When the rat finished, Ted turned to Bill. "While I don't agree with our unicycling Russian rat friend here that you are, in fact, a fucking douche-nozzle of the highest order, I have to say he's right that gambling is for idiots, and that you ought to know better." Buffalo Bill said his piece— or didn't, as reality would have it—and Ted turned back to Vladimir. It hadn't occurred to him that what he was doing bordered on insane; he just wanted to settle this argument so that he could disappear into the back room for a while, put the kettle on and work his way through a half-packet of Jammie Dodgers.

There was only one way to resolve this. Ted reached into his pocket and removed his wallet. He took out a crisp fiver and slammed it down on the shelf next to Vladimir. "Just take it," he said. "No… I am not paying the buffalo's debts for him, I am simply trying to be a good mediator… Well, that's your opinion, Vladimir, but might I suggest that, in future, you don't go lending money to a decapitated bison, and we wouldn't have this problem, would we?" A beat. "Right. That's settled it, then. Enjoy the rest of your day." To Bill he said, "You can go back to sleep now, and good luck with the horse thing. Hope it comes in for you."

He turned and headed for the counter at the opposite end of the shop, satisfied, smiling, happy to be alive.

Into the back room he went, and when he emerged five minutes later—cup of coffee in one hand and a quarter of a packet of Jammie Dodgers in the other— he saw he was no longer alone in the shop. Standing just beyond the counter were three men. Three impeccably-dressed men with dark, slicked-back hair. Ted didn't need to lean across the counter to know the men were wearing fancy Italian shoes costing more than his entire wardrobe. Their suits were sharp; the man in the middle, the shortest of the trio, wore a dark black Armani thingamajig while the pair flanking him had opted for grey two-pieces. When Ted saw them he almost dropped his biscuits.

"Oh! I didn't hear you come in!" Ted placed his coffee and biscuits down on the counter and adopted the 'I'm going to sell you something whether you like it or not' stance. "Take a look around, see if there's anything you fancy, and I'll just be here admiring your suits and wondering who your tailor is."

The one in the middle—who looked, Ted thought, a little like Marlon Brando in that film with the sleeping fishes—cracked a smile. "This fucking guy!" he said, turning to his buddies but motioning to Ted, who was already fishing a soggy biscuit from his coffee with two fingers. "This fucking guy cracks me up!"

The men either side of Brando laughed. It was so over the top and fake that Ted thought he had passed through some interdimensional portal and landed himself on the set of *Emmerdale*. He sucked the soggy biscuit from his burnt fingers and adopted the 'Okay, now I'm confused' stance, favoured by flustered politicians and Kardashians everywhere. "Erm, I'm sure something's funny," he said, "so why not share it with the rest of the class?"

"This fucking guy!" snorted the man in the middle.

"*This* fucking guy!" echoed the men either side of him in unison.

"Yeah, yeah, this fucking guy!" Ted said, becoming more frustrated. "Why are you all speaking in a silly Italian-American accent? This is Chiswick, is it not?"

"We're mafia," said the short-arse in the middle. "And you can't be mafia if you've got a cockney accent."

"But you're from round here?" Ted was perplexed, to say the least.

"Brentford," replied the henchmen, once again in unison. It was becoming terribly creepy.

"Brentford's lovely this time of year," Ted said, adopting his 'casual conversation' stance. "So you're not actually mafia, are you? You're just a trio of guys wearing fake tan and too much hair gel, dressed in expensive suits, putting on fake accents."

"This fucking guy!" said the one in the middle, leaning across the counter and slapping Ted twice, reasonably hard, across the chops. "Whether we are officially mafia is neither here nor there—"

"But you're not, though—"

"It's neither here nor there, you fucking old bastard. All you need to know is that you're dealing with Don Paparella"—he prodded himself in the chest with a thick tobacco-stained thumb— "Rocco 'Baby-Teeth' Gambone and Marco 'Thumbs' Arminio." He motioned to the men standing either side of him.

Ted turned his attention to the man on Paparella's left. "Why do they call you 'Baby-Teeth?'"

Baby-Teeth grinned to reveal a set of tiny pegs, the likes of which Ted had never seen before on anyone over the age of four.

"That makes perfect sense," Ted said. "The name, I mean, and not the fact that you probably struggle to eat anything harder than a rusk." He turned to the man on Don Paparella's right. "I take it they call you 'Thumbs' because you don't have any, right?"

Thumbs chortled, which wasn't in keeping with the mafia façade. "That's where you're wrong, buddy," he said, thrusting his hands into the air to reveal—

"Damn!" Ted gasped. "So you only have thumbs, absolutely no fingers, just a pair of huge thumbs! That's quite a curveball you're throwing people there."

"Okay, less of the chit-chat," Don Paparella said, adopting the 'I'm going to punch you in the face if you don't pack this nonsense in' stance. "You know our names, and you know that we're mafia—"

"But you're not, though—"

"I will cut your head off and shit down your neck if you interrupt me again, capiche?"

Ted had fairly had enough. How dare these people, these… *Brentonians* come into his shop and start threatening him. "Now you listen to me," he said. "I run a respectable business here, and I don't take kindly to threats from fake mafia…" He trailed off there, for he saw the gun emerge from Don Paparella's jacket pocket and surmised that it looked real enough.

"You were saying?" Don Paparella levelled the gun at Ted, who passed wind rather violently in response.

"Look, I don't want any trouble, okay? Just… just… take what you want, yeah, and then get the hell out of here. I'm just an old man trying to make a living out of dead things."

The three men who weren't mafia—had probably learned what they knew from *Goodfellas* and *Casino*—glanced around the shop, regarding the pieces with what appeared to be genuine disgust. "We don't want your dusty old buffalo heads, or your circus-freak rodents," said Don Paparella, scratching his temple with the barrel of the handgun. Ted was no firearms expert, but even he knew that was a silly thing to do. "We're actually here to offer *you* something, you lucky bastard."

Ted frowned. "Really?"

"Yeah." Don Paparella tucked the gun into the waistband of his trousers. Once again, Ted was no firearms expert, but he was pretty certain that was how ninety percent of sex-changes occurred. "We've extended the same offer, the offer we're going to make you right now, to your neighbours-in-trade, and they've all practically snatched our hands off."

Ted glanced down at Thumbs' fingerless hands, thought about cracking a joke and then decided against it.

"We're here to offer you protection in exchange for fifty percent of your takings," Don Paparella said. "Is that a fucking deal, or what!"

Ted almost choked on his own dentures. Half his takings? Fifty percent? An equal portion of BARKER'S STUFFED EMPORIUM (est. 1901 – We stuff things so you can stare at them forever!)? "No!" Ted said. "That's a terrible deal! And what could I possibly need 'protection' from, huh? The only customers I get are wealthy pet-owners or erudite gentlemen searching for something to brighten up the study wall."

Baby-Teeth cracked his knuckles, which would have been pretty menacing had he not whimpered in pain directly after.

"Let me put it another way," said Don Paparella, as calm as you like. "You're going to give us fifty percent of everything you make, and we're going to protect you from us. As I said, we have a special on at the moment. We'll throw in a whole year's membership to Paparella's Protection Services (we break kneecaps because we like to!), and your company will be safe from looters and thieves, ransackers and general wideboys. There is also an insurance element, in which you give us another three percent of your takings, and we definitely don't punch you in the throat for the first short week you hand us. After that, it's your funeral."

Ted stood there, incredulous, trying to figure out just how his day had gone from nondescript to just about as terrifying as possible. Once you got over the fake-tan, the fake mafia voices, and the ridiculous—and yet incredibly apt—monikers, it was easy to see that these were common crooks. Dangerous and stupid in equal measure. Malcolm Barker would turn in his grave if Ted accepted such godawful terms from a bunch of lunatics. The company wouldn't survive, for one. He was barely making enough to keep the lights on as it was, what with business rates rising quicker than Des O'Conner's blood pressure and the strange lull in city-centre footfall (which Ted thought might have something to do with the fact that ninety-eight percent of the shops were boarded up, and the other two percent were either electronic-cigarette vendors or stolen mobile phone unblocking services). On the bright side—if indeed there was one—fifty percent of hardly anything wouldn't amount to much.

Thank God for poor business!

"So what do I get out of it?" Ted said, reluctantly.

Don Paparella clicked his fingers and held his hand out, palm up and open. Into it, Baby-Teeth dropped what appeared to be a plastic keyring, which Don Paparella slammed down on the counter and slid across to Ted's side. "This magnificent plastic keyring could be yours if you sign the agreement"—he clicked his fingers once again and, as if by magic, a contract and a cheap pen (stolen from a bookies) appeared on the counter in front of Ted— "which cover everything I've just told you but in far less detail and with even more caveats. There's no point getting into the small print; it's far too small to read." He tapped impatiently upon the contract.

"This really does seem unfair," Ted ventured, glancing around at the contents of his shop. "The word 'extortion' springs to mind."

"We prefer to call it a 'shakedown'," Thumbs said. "Us Mafioso types don't know words like 'extortion'."

"Yeah," Baby-Teeth added. "We don't kill people either. We 'whack' them. I whacked a guy off just the other day—"

"Baby-Teeth!" Don Paparella shook his head. He turned back to Ted. "Sign the fucking paper, or I'll have no choice but to order one of my men to whack you off."

Ted dry-swallowed and picked up the stolen pen. He thought about the cricket bat sitting just beneath the counter, imagined grabbing it and swinging it at the

Brentford mafia, smashing their teeth out or, in the case of Baby-Teeth, knocking them back in. He thought about it, and yet he couldn't do it. These sonsofbitches meant business; he might take one of them out with his prized Ashes 2011 replica ball-whacker, but there were three of them, and the other two would no doubt punish him with a jolly good kicking. Or, even worse, he could be whacked off!

No, this was no time for heroics, which was just as well as the most heroic thing Ted Barker had ever done was cancel his home insurance.

He signed the contract, but not precisely on the dotted line. He wanted these fuckos to know he wasn't happy about this situation, that they were unable to faze him with threats of violence or whacking-off, and an intentionally misplaced signature seemed the right way to do that.

Don Paparella snatched up the signed contract and, after giving it the once over, stuffed it into his inside jacket pocket. "Thank you for choosing to take out a policy with Paparella's Protection Services (we take your money so you don't go spending it on things you don't really need!). We'll be collecting every Friday afternoon for the duration of your policy—which, if you'd taken time to read the impossible-to-read small print you'd know is fifty years or until death, whichever comes first—and *bada-bing, bada-bong,* if for some reason you've decided to go home early, Thumbs here will make sure that upon your return you'll find a pile of ashes where your shop used to sit."

As if to prove just how serious he was, Marco 'Thumbs' Arminio produced a lighter and flicked the switch. Luckily, it was one of those thumb-operated ones. A flame appeared for a split-second, but was gone just as fast. "I think I need a new lighter, boss," he groaned, working at the flint. "How am I supposed to torch anything with this dodgy thing?"

"We'll get you a new lighter this afternoon," Don Paparella sighed. "Honestly, I can't take you two anywhere without it costing me an arm and a leg." He turned his attention back to Ted, who was still considering reaching for the cricket bat. "If it's not new lighters, it's 'Can I have an ice-cream, boss?' or 'I need a wee, boss, and I can't hold it.' No wonder I'm the made guy around here."

"But you're not, though," Ted said. "I've got a cheese and ham pizza in my fridge more Italian than you."

Don Paparella moved so quickly that he became a blur, and then Ted was screaming, and wondering just how that stolen pen had managed to stab itself in the back of his hand. He quickly reached for it, pulled it out, watched as the blood geysered up for a moment before trying to decide whether he should pass out or not.

"Did that hurt?" Paparella asked, a slight smirk curling his lips up. "You're lucky I'm in a good fucking mood today, Mister Barker. However, come Friday, you'd better have something for me, or you'll find out what I'm like when I'm in a bad mood."

"It ain't pleasant," Baby-Teeth said.

Don Paparella picked up the plastic keyring and dropped it into his pocket. "You don't deserve a nice plastic keyring," he said. "Now who's laughing, huh."

Ted sucked at the blood pouring from the back of his hand, his mouth filling with a coppery bitterness. Was it possible to die from a pen to the hand? "Is it possible to die from a pen to the hand?"

"I don't think so," Paparella said, though he didn't look too sure. "I've never heard of anyone dying from a pen to the hand, but then again I've never heard of anyone dying from a stick of asparagus to the anus either, but that doesn't mean it couldn't happen."

"We should go, boss," Thumbs said, motioning to the door. "We've got that electronic cigarette kiosk across the road to shake down, and then three more stolen mobile phone unblocking shops."

"Not enough hours in the day," Paparella said, somewhat sadly. "Any-hoo, it's been an absolute pleasure signing you up for a policy, and we're truly glad we didn't have to whack you off."

"I'm sure it wouldn't have been *that* bad," Ted said, for he hadn't been whacked off in many a year.

"Right!" Don Paparella rubbed his hands together like a villain from a Bond film. "Come on, you two. Busy day ahead, and standing here in this animal graveyard isn't making money, now, is it?" He turned and marched toward the door. Thumbs and Baby-Teeth followed. Thumbs whistled the *Godfather* theme tune as he went, which might or might not have been in his contract.

"Can we have an ice-cream, boss?" Baby-Teeth said, holding the door open for his capo. Don Paparella slapped him hard in the face and continued out onto the street.

Then they were gone, leaving Ted Barker standing there behind his counter wondering what the hell had just happened. In the distance, he thought he heard a groan and a shuffle, the sound of his father and his grandfather turning in their respective graves.

4

By the time Ted arrived at The Swan with Three Tits (get pissed, pay your tab, and get out!) he had calmed down a little. There was no way he was handing those mafia bozos half his takings. Not a chance, nope, not on your nelly. He would rather eat his own eyelashes than pay for protection from a trio of faux Italian-Americans from Brentford.

Protection?

What, in the name of Christ and all that was good and pure, could they possibly protect him from? His clientele was hardly the violent type; no one ever smashed through the front window of his shop, leapt in wearing a motorcycle jacket and a balaclava, wielding an axe or shotgun, and ordered Ted to "put the fez-wearing squirrel in the bag and no one gets hurt." It just didn't happen. That's not to say it *couldn't* happen. There was always a chance, much like there was always a chance Professor Stephen Hawking would, one day, suddenly spring from his chair and burst into an energetic rendition of *Singing in the Rain* whilst throwing himself bodily around the place. It was possible, but not fucking likely.

"How's it going, Ted? Looking a bit flustered there, mate. What can I get you? The usual? Two of the usual? A whole plethora of the usual and keep them coming until we have to peel you up off the carpet?" Jasper Quim was a good landlord, the best The Swan had ever had, but he didn't half go on a bit.

"The last one please, Quimmy," Ted said, settling himself upon a stool at the bar, which wobbled precariously beneath him. All of the stools in The Swan with Three Tits were the same: dangerous, ripped, a claims company's wet dream. Once you got the hang of them, though, knew which ones would result in an afternoon flicking through ancient *National Geographic* magazines and waiting for some prick to call your name out in A&E, you were alright.

Jasper set about pouring Ted his usual—triple scotch on the rocks—and talked as he did so. "So what's the matter, Ted? Just realised that all of your pets are dead and are now staring out at you through sad, glass eyes?" He laughed; Ted didn't.

"I think I've made a terrible mistake," Ted said,

drumming his fingers nervously upon the sticky—and frankly downright filthy—counter. He reached unconsciously for the peanut bowl to his right, saw what could only be described as a cluster of pubic hairs nestled in amongst the nuts, and quickly changed his mind.

"We all make mistakes, Ted," Jasper said as he presented Ted with his usual. "I've been married twice, remember?"

Ted shook his head. "That's not too bad," he said.

"The second time was to a racehorse named Sherguff." Jasper held his hand out, and Ted placed a crusty five-pound note into it. "See, what I'm saying is that everyone is entitled to mess up every now and then. Never, since that second divorce, have I mistakenly in the eyes of the law become contractually united with an equine beast. Once is enough…"

"Once is still a bit weird," Ted opined.

"You live and learn," Jasper countered.

"I learnt not to marry horses many moons ago." Ted picked up his glass and swallowed half of it in a single gulp. Hissing as the burn arrived at his stomach, he said, "No, I had a little visit today from a couple of ne'er-do-wells, and it's shook me up a little. To be honest, I haven't yet come to terms with the enormity of what I've done."

Jasper smiled knowingly. "Signed half your business away have you to a trio of fake Italian-Americans from Brentford?" He clicked his tongue and rolled his eyes, and other things of that genuine nature.

Ted was shell-shocked. "You know about them?" he said. "About Don Paparella and the one with the baby-teeth and the one with only thumbs on his hands, when his name tricks you into believing that his thumbs are the digits that have been removed?"

"*Know* about them?" Jasper said, wiping at a clean glass with a dirty rag. "I took out two policies with them just this very afternoon."

It took Ted a while to absorb what Quimmy was telling him, but when he did, he said, "Hang on a minute. You took two policies out with them? As in two different contracts?"

Jasper shook his head. "*Same* contract, just… *two* of them."

"But that contract was for *half* of your takings, Quimmy," Ted said, exasperatedly knocking back the remains of his scotch. He slammed the empty glass down on the counter and Jasper set about refilling it. "If you've signed two of them, you're going to give them a hundred percent of your takings. What will you *live* on?"

"My unshattered kneecaps," Jasper said. "I thought they were very reasonable terms. You don't know how important kneecaps are until they're no longer there. Thankfully—thanks to Don Paparella—I'll never have to worry about losing mine."

This was madness! Absolute madness! Ted couldn't just let this happen. "I can't let this happen!" he said.

"This is madness! Absolute madness!"

"Calm your tits, Ted," Jasper said. "It's not just us those Mafioso types paid a visit to. You're the tenth person I've spoken to today who was strong-armed into signing a contract. Dave from Mobile Phone Unlockers Ltd. signed one, as did Phil from the UK Phone Unlocking Warehouse. Beth from E-Cigs R Us refused to sign, so she's in hospital now having an electronic cigarette removed from her derriere, so once news of that got out people were pretty keen to take out a policy."

"This is a joke!" Ted said, though if it were, he was clearly missing the punchline. *Three fake gangsters from Brentford walk into a taxidermist's…* nope, he had nothing. "We have to go to the police, Quimmy. We have to stop these… these…" He wanted to say *badfellas*, but it was a terrible joke and now was not the time.

"The police already know about them," Jasper said, resuming his glass-polishing.

"Oh," Ted said. "Oh, well, that's good, I suppose."

"Not really," said Jasper. "Don Paparella is now getting half of the money the police make from fines. Think about that the next time you drop litter." He laughed, though there was more than a modicum of sadness in there.

Ted couldn't believe what he was hearing, that these arseholes were getting away with what could only be described as mass-extortion. And instead of doing something about it, the police—the people tasked with making the community a safe place for all—had signed on the dotted line, the same as everyone else. "Well, if no one else is going to put their foot down, *I* bloody well will." He knocked back his second scotch so fast it barely touched the sides. "I might be an old man, but there's plenty of fight still left in these old limbs."

Jasper looked unsure as he filled Ted's glass for a third time. "What are you going to do, Ted? Nothing stupid, I hope. I don't want to have to come visit you in hospital while the surgeons work out how best to remove a stoat-in-a-bikini from your back passage."

Ted winced, for that was a sentence he never thought he would hear. "Okay, bear with me." He pushed himself up from the wobbly stool, and then proceeded to climb up onto it, using the counter to steady himself.

"That's not a good idea," Jasper said, leaning across to prevent Ted from toppling back., for he knew down there, on the beer-sticky and fag-ash-singed carpet lay certain death for a man of Ted's age and wiriness. "Come on down, Ted, you've already had a few to drink and—"

"No!" Ted said, pulling himself up to standing. "This needs to be said. These people need a leader, Quimmy, and I am *him*… I am *he*… I am, how would you say it?"

"I wouldn't," Jasper said.

"Right!" Ted stepped across onto the bar and turned to face the myriad drinkers, the fruit-machine gamblers, the currently-out-of-workers, and the borderline alcoholics. He cleared his throat, and that was when a tomato hit him in the forehead. Jasper urged people not to throw fruit or vegetables at the madman standing upon the bar, and the contents of The Swan with Three Tits fell silent as they eagerly anticipated what would come next.

"Aren't you Doctor Doolittle?" said one man from the back of the pub. "The one what talks to his stuffed animals?"

"Leave 'im alone!" a fabulously unkempt woman screeched in what could only be described as witch-voice. "'E fixed my frog, 'e did. Croaker's never looked so bleedin' smart in 'is tuxedo."

"Ladies and gentlemen," Ted said, teetering on the edge of the bar and almost putting his foot through the pubic-hair peanuts. "Ladies and gentlemen, this is important, so if you could just bear with me for a moment. It involves all of us, all of you, wonderful people of Chiswick—"

"I've got a cat at home," said the rude man once again. "You want me to go fetch it so it can hear your oh-so-important announcement?"

"Knock it off, Roger," Jasper said as he added a fresh handful of pubes to the bar snacks. "Let the man talk, or you're barred until further notice." Which meant— Ted knew, as he had been barred until further notice many times—Roger would be allowed back in in half an hour, so long as he behaved himself and put a quid in the tip-jar.

Ted ignored the man and continued with what would

hopefully be a rousing speech. Or not. "Ladies and gentlemen, earlier today, as did some of you, I received a visit from three men dressed in fine suits and sharp shoes. Despite their awful fake mafia dialect and stereotypical demeanours—usually a sign that someone is taking the piss—it quickly became clear, when one of them pulled a gun on me, that they were to be taken very seriously, unless one wanted a smoking hole in the front of one's face. Now, those of you who have businesses will know that things are a little tight at the moment, and that we can barely afford to keep paying the exorbitant rates to the council, let alone feed our children so that their ribcages remain on the inside."

"By *children*, you mean that two-headed duck you've got in your window?" Roger couldn't help himself.

"Right, Roger, out!" Jasper said, marching around the bar and motioning to the door. "You can come back in half-an-hour, or when Ted's finished his rant, whichever comes first."

Roger skulked from the pub, shaking his head and cursing under his breath. And what terrible breath it was, too.

Ted, happy now that his heckler had been banished, continued. "We cannot allow our livelihoods, or at least fifty percent of them, to fall into the hands of these… these pretend wiseguys—"

"Try telling that to Beth from E-Cigs R Us," said a voice from the middle of the room. Ted glanced around, spotted the speaker amongst the throng: Martin

Chuzzlechops, the village idiot. Martin was the kind of guy you could sell bottled air to, even if the cap was missing.

"Yes, these are violent men," Ted said, once again addressing the entire audience. "Yes, they have no qualms in shoving things up people's bottoms, and yes, there will probably be more trips to A&E to remove said things from our bottoms until we, by way of protest, show these lunatics that we will not be pushed around. That we will not allow them to come into our places of business and steal the money from our tills and the stale Cornish pasties from our hands. We will not stand idly by while the shirts are ripped from our backs and the trousers are slid over our emaciated legs."

"But we signed contracts," Jasper Quim said, drinking vodka directly from its bottle. "Some of us signed two of the bastards."

Ted nodded. "Yes, but what are contracts other than pieces of paper with long and boring sections of incomprehensible law-speak followed by a short, but equally ineligible, paragraph of small-print where they hide all the stuff you really don't want to be reading?"

"Legally binding?" said the witch, Caroline Munster. She followed this up with a cackle, simply to remain in character.

"Well, *yes*," Ted said, suddenly unsure of where he had been going with his diatribe. "Look, we're all in this together, and if those sonsofbitches want a war, then they'll get one. Who's with me?" He punched the air with a white-knuckled fist. A fly, which had been minding its own business and waiting for someone to change the peanuts in the bowl on the bar, dropped to the carpet, dazed and confused.

Martin Chuzzlechops threw his hand in the air. "I'm with you!" he said, much to the chagrin of those standing around him, who whispered and tsked and things of that general nature. A tomato thumped into Martin's back; Caroline Munster, grinning, was in the process of reloading with a cabbage.

"Oh, come on!" Ted said, incredulous. "People, did you not hear my wonderful speech? Did it not raise the hackles on your necks and the peckers in your pants?"

"Time to get down, Ted," Jasper said, nodding to the ground. "You tried—can't say you didn't try—but these people aren't fighters. This isn't *Braveheart*, and you sure as hell ain't Mel Gibson."

"I'll be taking that one as a compliment," Ted said, climbing down from the bar. The people of the pub were already moving on, returning to their drinks, their crisps and cheese-and-onion cobs, their drinking buddies or AA sponsors. "I can't believe this, Quimmy. We won't last a year. They're going to take, take, take, and when there's nothing left to take… well, we'll probably be dead by that point, or living on Super Noodles and drinking shaving foam straight from the can."

"I think you're making a mountain out of a mole-hill," Jasper said, now polishing a clean glass with an old sock.

"But I don't have a bloody mole-hill, do I, Quimmy? I have half a bloody mole-hill, and guess who's got the other half? Those wiseguy *wankers*, that's who, and I'll tell you another thing…" But Ted stopped there, for Jasper Quim was frantically shaking his strangely-shaped head and his eyes were wider than saucers. "What's the matter with you, Quimmy?" Ted said. "Is this some sort of seizure? Do I have to locate a special injection or anything upon your person?" But Jasper Quim was not, in fact, in the throes of an epileptic fit, as Ted quickly realised when a voice from behind said:

"This fucking guy!"

Ted dry-swallowed, for he knew that voice, that fake Italian-American accent which sounded like Don Corleone channelled by Dick Van Dyke. And then a huge pair of thumbs slammed down onto the bar to Ted's right before stirring the pubic-hair peanuts in an attempt to find one yet to be tainted.

Jasper, suddenly nervous, regarded Don Paparella with an amalgamation of contempt and respect—fifty percent 'I fucking hate you' and fifty percent 'I hate you, but I like my kneecaps'. "Hey… erm… Don," Jasper said. "Can I call you Don? Is that okay? I mean, I wouldn't want to—"

"You can call me whatever the fuck you like so long as you've got my money, capiche?" Don Paparella plonked himself down on the stool next to Ted; Baby Teeth stood just behind, guarding over his capo, making sure no one threw a cabbage at him, no doubt. "So, business is looking good." Paparella motioned to the heaving pub. "You know, this is the first public house I've ever owned outright. I mean, yeah, there have been strip clubs, and casinos, and nightclubs, but never any real British pubs. Until now."

"You're very welcome," Jasper said, stuttering ever-so-slightly. "Can I get you a drink, Don? Perhaps your enormous henchmen would like a lemonade spritzer. On the house, of course."

"Scotch," Paparella said. "No ice… little umbrella… two cherries… one straw… in a pint glass… with a handle on the side."

Jasper nodded far too much for Ted's liking before setting about preparing Paparella's ridiculous drink. "Anything for the minions?"

"Do you have those little blackcurrant Fruit Shoots?" Paparella asked. Jasper nodded. "Two of those, then, and a couple of packets of Jelly Babies."

Thumbs clapped excitedly, although it wasn't much of a clap; more of a tapping together of two oversized digits.

With Jasper busy, Ted soon felt eyes boring into him, and so it wasn't much of a surprise when he glanced across and saw Don Paparella staring back, grinning, trying to pull a recalcitrant pube from between his chemically-whitened teeth. "Don't try the nuts," the capo said. "They're far more work than it's worth."

"I'll bear that in mind," Ted said, unsure of where to

look.

"Hey, you're the guy who owns half of that place in town! The taxidermy place. Yeah, I remember you now. Got some great little pieces in that shop of ours, don't we? All those stuffed animals… you truly are an artist, *Barker*, is it?"

Ted nodded, though he hated being called by just his last name. That was how Hitler became such a hated figure.

"Never been an animal-lover myself," Paparella said, slipping in and out of his fake accent more times than Katie Price slipped out of her knickers. "It's the fur, you see. Goes right through me, it does. And don't even get me started on the fucking noise they make! I swear to fucking Christ, back home in Brooklyn, my Mama's house, we had these neighbours who just fucking loved cats. I mean they loved them so much, you couldn't fit another one in their house if you tried."

Jasper placed a pint glass filled with scotch down on the bar—looking resplendent with its miniature umbrella and cherry embellishments—along with a pair of blackcurrant Fruit Shoots. "We're out of straws," he said. "I'm so sorry, Don Paparella. Does this mean you'll be wanting to put my head in a vise and turn the handle until my eyes pop out?"

Paparella sighed. "Maybe later," he said. "Anyway, these cats, these fucking *cats*, they pissed and shit everywhere, and I mean every-fucking-where. There was shit in our mailbox, in Mama's best slippers, in our *toilet.* Can you fucking *believe* that? Cat shit in our human fucking toilet?"

Ted shook his head. "That's just awful," he said.

"Right? So in the end, me and my brother, Tiny Paparella—big guy, older than me—we decided to do something about it. So one day, when Mama was asleep, we snuck out, and do you know what we did?"

"I'm guessing you killed the cats," Ted said, motioning to his empty glass. Jasper refilled it, and Ted knocked it back in one go.

Don Paparella shrugged. "Sure, we could have done *that*, but no. We knocked on our neighbour's door and, when she answered—old lady, looked a little like a cat herself—we said, 'Any chance you could stop your cats from shitting in our human toilet?'" He settled back on his stool, which was a silly thing to do as it didn't have a back to it. When he picked himself up from the sticky carpet a few seconds later—aided by his Fruit Shoot-drinking lackeys—he said, "And it worked. No more cat shit in our human toilet, and no one had to get whacked off."

If there was a point to the story, Ted must have missed it.

"You're thinking that if there's a point to this story, then you must have missed it," Paparella said, rather shrewdly. "But there is a point. The point is, you don't have to kill a houseful of cats unless it's absolutely necessary, and that, my friend, is why you'd better not renege on our deal, because I will set fire to your tail and pull your whiskers out quicker than you can say 'Help, I'm just a lowly taxidermist!', do you fucking understand me?"

"Sort of," Ted said. "Do you know any good jokes?" A change of subject seemed to be the best course of action.

"Jokes? What am I? A clown? Here to fucking amuse you?"

Ah, Ted thought. *Should have seen that one coming.*

"Now, me and my boys are going to shoot some pool," Paparella said, picking up his glass from the bar. "I'm glad we had this little chat. Since we're business partners, and suchlike. Enjoy the rest of your evening, but make sure you're open on time first thing in the morning. We're not going to make much money if you're lying in bed with a terrible hangover, now, are we?"

Ted forced a smile as the Brentford Bandits made their way across the pub to where three chavs were trying to figure out which of them would be playing the winner. It turned out that none of them would as Don Paparella snatched the pool cue from the biggest chav and cracked it over his head. A brawl ensued, however it was the most one-sided fight in the history of brawls, since none of the chavs were willing to fight back. One of them even went so far as to throw *himself* through the window.

Ted placed his head in his hands and said, "Another scotch please, Quimmy, and better make it a triple-

triple."

"I'm out of scotch," Jasper said, polishing a light-bulb with a pair of old lady's pants. "Don had the last bottle. Might I tempt you with a Tom Collins?"

"A Tom Collins?" Ted said. "Isn't that scotch, lemon, and ice?"

"Let me rephrase it," Jasper said. "Would you like some lemon with ice?"

Ted climbed down from his stool and took out his wallet. A moth flew out—something Ted thought only happened in Disney cartoons—and would have made it to the light-bulb in Jasper's hand had it not been for the 8-ball flying through the air at close to the speed of light. The moth disintegrated instantly, and the 8-ball buried itself in the dart board. "No, I've got a lot of work to do tomorrow," he said, thinking about the suave fox he would be creating and mounting. "I've got to mount a monocle- and waistcoat-wearing fox first thing."

"Each to their own," Jasper said. "Takes all sorts, I suppose," he added. "Whatever floats your b—"

"Yes, that's quite enough of that nonsense," Ted said. "Enjoy the rest of your evening, Quimmy. Hope you're still alive tomorrow."

"You too, Ted," Jasper said.

Ted left The Swan with Three Tits in a worse mood than when he went in. He stepped over the moaning chav with bits of glass in his face and headed for home.

5

It was a pleasant day, or as pleasant as one could expect it to be in mid-May. Ted had dealt with precisely one customer, a cantankerous old biddy whose cat, Devereaux, had taken it upon itself to play chicken with a train. "Lady," Ted had told her as she'd unveiled what remained of her beautiful moggie. "I am a taxidermist, not a magician."

"So are you saying that you can't fix him?" the woman had dejectedly enquired.

"You might as well have brought me a two-slice toaster," Ted had told her, for a two-slice toaster would have had exactly the same number of legs as the thing laid out before him. "I'm really sorry, but the best thing you can do for Devereaux right now is… well, set fire to him."

"I don't believe in cremation," the woman had said, stuffing the squashed feline worm back into her handbag.

"Then bury the poor thing in your garden," Ted had replied.

"Don't have a garden," the woman had said, zipping her handbag up. "Live in a flat."

"Then throw it out of the window of your flat," Ted had said, fairly losing his rag. "Really, lady, I don't know what else to tell you."

"You're a very rude man, Mister Barker," the woman had said, shuffling toward the door like Yoda in a headscarf. *A very rude man, you are.* "I hope those gangsters remove your kneecaps so that you walk like an ostrich for the rest of your life." And with that she was gone.

And with that, Ted was left with a terrible taste in his mouth. The woman had reminded him about Don Paparella and his henchmen, Tweedle-Thumb and Tweedle-Teeth. He had managed to work through the entire morning, putting the finishing touches to a rather eloquent fox, without once thinking of the Brentford mafia, or what they would do to him when they visited him that very same day, only to discover that Ted had had second thoughts about the whole thing, that he had signed the contract accidentally, and that it wasn't worth the paper it was printed on, mainly because he had been so nervous and shaky at the time that the signature looked nothing like his, and was therefore probably inadmissible in court.

In the studio at the rear of the shop, Ted stood admiring his handiwork, still nervous about Don Paparella, but doing everything he could to push it from his mind.

The fox—tartan waistcoat, pocketwatch, monocle, all the accoutrements of a dickhead—stood on its hind legs and seemed to regard Ted with a mixture of gratitude and contempt. *Thanks for giving me life, but you could have made me a little bit less of a nonce.*

"It's going to be a bad day, Mister Fox," Ted said, turning his creation around to make sure the tail hadn't drooped, a common fault with poncy foxes. "But somebody has to stand up them. We can't just let them get away with this. It's theft of the highest order! I haven't felt this violated since my last prostate exam. At least I got a lollypop out of that."

The fox spoke to him in such a wonderfully treacly voice, posh and verbose, that Ted felt instantly better about his predicament.

"Why yes!" Ted replied, running a hand through what remained of his silver hair. "Very nice of you to say so. I don't believe in toupees. Could you imagine me with a wig?"

The fox spoke again—or didn't, as reality would have it.

"Yes, I guess I do look a little like a white Morgan Freeman," Ted said, though he thought the fox was just being polite, as was its wont. "Look, Mister Fox… I don't feel comfortable calling you that. It's ridiculous. You sound like something out of a Beatrix Potter porn parody. What's your real name?"

A few seconds passed as the fox apparently considered a pseudonym, and only after a little coaxing from Ted did the new creation offer up his real name.

"*Fairfax!*" Ted said, clapping his hands together in delight. "That's a marvellous name, for such a marvellous creature. I should imagine you know the Queen, Fairfax, with a name like that… Oh, you do! She used to feed you the bones of her deceased corgis! One would expect nothing less of Her Maj." He stood back and admired Fairfax in all his resplendence. Such a shame he would have to be sold; Ted hated the fact he couldn't afford to hold on to his creations after all the work he put into them—all the stuffing he put into them. Business was business, though, and Fairfax, the cheeky little scamp, would probably go for three- or four-hundred pound, if the right customer came in. Two-hundred pound if Ted got desperate or the electricity was cut off again.

"Well, it's been an absolute delight working on you," Ted said, picking the whole thing up by its wooden mount. "I hope it wasn't too uncomfortable… Oh, yes, I do have small hands for a man, I suppose… yes, well, I clip them regularly… I always worry that you poor animals have already been through the wringer, what with recently dying and stuff, and the last thing you want is for some talon-ed maniac putting his hand up inside you and rearranging your giblets." He carried Fairfax through to the shop, where he would take pride of place in the window. A whole display would be built around the fox. A tea-party, perhaps, or a masked ball, one of those ones which ninety percent of the time ended up in a giant orgy.

That was the plan, at least, but when Ted stepped through into the shop, he knew his plans were about to change.

"This fucking guy!" Don Paparella said. He was standing at the counter, flicking through Ted's books. Ted hadn't felt so violated since his last prostate…

never mind. "You know what day it is?"

Ted, suddenly aware of how heavy Fairfax was, slowly walked to the counter and placed the fox down. "I know what day it is," he said.

Don Paparella, flanked by his lackeys, examined the fox with something akin to confusion etched across their countenances. "You know," the capo said, "I've never understood why anyone would do this to an animal. A fucking majestic fox like this, and what's it reduced to?" Then he was talking directly to Fairfax, and Ted didn't like that one bit. "Mister Fox like to hang around school playgrounds, huh? Mister Fox an ice-cream man, huh? Look at you, you poor sonofabitch. Is that a fucking monocle? Can you believe this shit? Mister Barker's decked a fucking fox out in a waistcoat and jabbed a monocle into its fucking eye! And *we're* the monsters!"

Fairfax said something that only Ted could hear, and Ted stifled a laugh.

"Something funny, Mister Barker?" Thumbs asked.

"You ask permission to stifle a laugh in front of Don Paparella," Baby-Teeth added. "Capiche?"

Ted composed himself. To the capo he said, "I see you've already taken a good look at the books. You are therefore aware of the unfortunate shortfall this week."

Don Paparella nodded. "Yeah. I saw all those blank pages, and I thought 'this can't be the fucking books! What's with all these blank pages, followed by one page at the back which consists entirely of doodle penises?'

That's not very professional, not at all."

Clearing his throat, Ted decided to take a little walk around the shop. He felt three pairs of eyes following him, watching him closely, making sure he didn't make any sudden moves. What was he going to do? Beat them to death with a rat on a unicycle? "I'm afraid there has been a change of plan," Ted said, his heart racing so fast it was audible to all present. "You see, I'm a hardworking citizen, and I believe I was strong-armed into signing that contract." He turned to Hooter, who said something awfully racist about the three fake gangsters and described, in no small detail, what they could do with their meatballs. "Taxidermy is a dying trade, Don Paparella. There are fewer and fewer of us with each generation—respectable artists, I mean, not those arseholes churning out mass-produced basses or pipistrelle bats pinned to dartboards." He moved across to where Jemima/Jessica stood; the girls were unusually quiet, given the circumstances. "But artist, such as myself, can't compete with those charlatans, those men who learned the trade watching videos on the YouTube, or whatever the hell it's called."

Marco 'Thumbs' Arminio slipped a hand into his jacket pocket, as if to retrieve something—a *gun*—but Paparella shook his head. He needn't have bothered, as Thumbs took out an ice lolly in the shape of a human foot and began licking around its toes. Paparella shook his head and turned his attention back to Ted.

"I guess what I'm trying to say," Ted said, "is that

there is no money here for you, nor will there be tomorrow, or the day after. And while I respect you—inasmuch as you have weapons and I really have no other choice—this is one taxidermist who will *not* acquiesce to your demands, who will *not* genuflect as you waltz in here as if you own the place, who will *not* be handing you a brown envelope on a Friday afternoon filled with his hard-earned cash, and that, Don Paparella, is the way it is."

God, he felt so *good*. So terribly scared, and yet relieved. He had said his piece, and it was a piece he had been practising for many hours, and not once had he stuttered or faltered. It had come out strong, intense; the sermon couldn't have been better if Christopher Walken had delivered it.

"That was... beautiful," Paparella said, wiping an invisible tear from the corner of his eye. "You got balls, old man. Big balls. Big hairy balls covered in hair and shaped like balls."

Ted watched as Thumbs bit three toes from his ice-lolly before throwing the rest of it across the room. It stuck, somewhat fortuitously, to Fairfax's face.

Don Paparella was applauding now. Slow-clapping. Sarcastic. "You know what that reminded me of?" he said. "That reminded me of that movie... what was it called...? Help me out here, boys."

"*Antz*," Baby-Teeth said.

"*The Brave Little Toaster*," Thumbs added.

"Youse guys are a fucking joke," Paparella said.

"Unless Christopher Walken was in *Antz*—"

"He *was*, boss!" Baby-Teeth said. "He played Colonel Cutter, General Mandible's right-hand-man—"

"I will shoot you in the fucking face if you keep talking," Paparella interrupted, and now he had a gun in his hand, and it was a big gun and looked very much like the real thing. Baby-Teeth fell quiet, for he knew that his capo meant it. "This fucking guy!" he said, turning to Ted and levelling the gun at him. He grinned, and it was positively shark-like—the grin of a man who should come with his own theme-music. *Dah-dum… dah-dum… dum-dum-dum-duh…* or something like that. "As I was saying, you got balls, old man, but unfortunately you signed that contract the same as every other business in this fucking neighbourhood. There's only one way you're getting out of this deal, and if you're telling me that it's a shitty deal—for *me*—and that I'm not gonna make any money out of you, then I'm gonna turn this place into a mobile-phone unlocking centre or electronic cigarette shop and make money out of it thataway."

Ted took a tentative step back; the chamber of the gun followed him.

"I guess what I'm saying is that you're no good to me alive," Paparella said.

He pulled the trigger.

And for Ted Barker, everything went black.

6

The shop was quiet. Not just quiet, but supernaturally silent, as if the whole room had been suddenly submerged underwater. The trio of killers had only been gone for a couple of minutes, and yet time passed slowly in BARKER'S STUFFED EMPORIUM. Minutes felt like hours, and hours felt like days, so in a roundabout way, and if you were clever enough to do the maths, minutes felt like days, and yet Ted Barker remained unmoving on the floor, blood blossoming out from his head and pooling beneath him.

The bullet had gone straight through Barker's skull, had embedded itself in the wall just above Vladimir the Unicycling Rat. It was all very messy. Soon, Ted Barker would only be a chalk line—and no one ever wanted to end up as a chalk line—and soon after, not even that.

Silence.

More silence.

Yet more silence.

If this were a film, the audience would be getting wound up by now.

And then, something could be heard. A shrill squeak, a plaintive keen, a melancholy hoot, an elegiac whine. A voice said, "They shot him! The bloody fake Ities shot his head off!" It had come from the owl—Hooter—but that wasn't possible, was it? Owls don't talk; you're lucky if you get a 'Who' out of them, aren't you?

"No!" said another voice, this one from the shelf

across the room, the shelf upon which a unicycling rat was now tottering back and forth on his tiny one-wheeled contraption. "No! He's not dead! He's our father, he can't be dead!"

Hanging upon the wall, the mouth of the buffalo head—Bill—dropped open. A deep sound issued from within, a sonorous moan, and then it said, "This can't be happening. This isn't happening."

"Oh, it's happening alright," said a female voice on the other side of the room. And then a second female voice said, "What do *you* fucking know? You don't know everything, you quacking slut. You've never seen a dead man before—"

"I know a dead man when I see one!" gasped Jemima, one half of the two-headed duck. "My first clue was when his head came off."

"Oh, so she's a CSI investigator, all of a sudden," Jessica said, sarcastically.

"Ladies, ladies, ladies," said the baby giraffe at the edge of the room. "This isn't the time to argue, yeah? Our creator's lying dead with bits of his face… oh, dear me, there are bits of his face on *my* face. I think I'm going to be sick."

"Does anyone have a serviette?" said Fairfax the Fox, shaking the half-melted strawberry ice-lolly from his face. "One is awfully sticky."

"Oh, newbie's only worried about bit of ice-lolly in fur," said Vladimir the Unicycling Rat in broken English. "Father lies dead in middle of shop and stupid fox complains about stickiness."

A tongue flicked out of Fairfax's mouth and lapped at the pink goo around its maw. When he had licked most of the mess away, he said, in a voice which would have made Hugh Grant sound like a hobo from Hackney, "One is terribly sorry about the loss of this poor, poor fellow, however my memories of said dead man are sketchy, to say the least. One does recall a moment, not terribly long ago, in which the man before me shoved four fingers and a thumb into one's back-passage and stretched one's inner cavity out. Ah," he sighed. "Such fond reminiscences."

"Listen, gingerbollocks," said Hooter, his head spinning all the way round so that he could better see the posh fox. "You show some respect when you're talking about that man. If it wasn't for him, you'd still be at the side of a road somewhere, half-eaten by flies and badgers."

Fairfax smiled slightly, but foxes always do, don't they? Usually before they rape your cat or take a hulking shit in your outdoor shoes. "Please, forgive me," said the fox. "One didn't mean to offend. Allow me to introduce myself. I am Fairfax, most dapper fox this side of the Thames—"

"You're a dickhead," Hooter said. "Now, please let us mourn in peace. A minute's silence is in order for the brave man who now lies upon the shop floor."

"Some of him is lying on my face," said Gerry the Giraffe.

"Well shake it off, then!" Buffalo Bill said, his voice so deep that, three miles away, an old man achieved his first orgasm in over thirty years, and he wasn't even playing with it.

Gerry shook his head and a knob of flesh—once Ted Barker's left eyebrow—dropped to the wooden plinth beneath him with a thump.

"Minute silence," said Vladimir. "We have to pay tribute to great man."

"He was no great man!" quacked Jemima. "He was a selfish old so-and-so who didn't want to sell any of us on, just in case, God forbid, we would be happier elsewhere."

"Ignore her," said Jessica. "She's just pissed that she's the extra head, and I'm the real head."

"You are not the real head. This is my body. You are trespassing!"

"Look at the way you're leaning to the side!" Jessica countered. "Anyone with eyes can see that you don't belong on this body, that you were put here by a man having a mid-life crisis. I bet if I lift up your feathers we'll see the stitches—"

"You'd better not *touch* my feathers, you harlot!" Jemima screeched. "I'll peck your damn eyes out!"

"My," said Fairfax, licking his lips. "what wonderful ladies."

"You'd better stay the hell away from me!" Jessica told Fairfax. "But feel free to chew Jemima's head off, since it's NOT MEANT TO BE THERE IN THE

FIRST PLACE!"

"Ridiculous!" mumbled Vladimir, almost falling off the shelf upon which he tottered. "Absolute ridiculous!"

"Everyone just calm down," Hooter said, opening his wings for the first time in a week. "We're going to get through this minute's silence if it kills us."

"Is that all we're going to do for him?" asked Gerry. "A minute's silence? After he gave us life after death, we're going to repay him with sixty seconds of not talking?"

Silence. Gerry had a point. For a baby giraffe, he was a clever one.

"Gerry is right," said Vladimir. "We can't let this go. Those… those maniacs kill him, kill our creator. We must revenge him."

"Avenge," Hooter said. "It's 'avenge', not 'revenge', you dumb Russki rodent."

"Vladimir has a point," said Bill, nodding toward the still-twitching corpse of Ted Barker. "They gunned him down in cold blood, but they didn't consider the fact that there were witnesses."

"Spiffing!" said Fairfax. "A retaliation! One can barely contain one's foxy cry… no, here it comes… eeeeeeeeeeeeeeeeeeeeEEEEEEEEEEEEE!"

"Shut up, you fool!" Hooter said. Fairfax fell silent. "You're not one of us. You're new here, your stuffing hasn't even had a chance to settle yet. You're an immigrant, and nothing more."

"How very date you," Fairfax said, clearly annoyed. "One was born in London, and one spent one's entire life riffling through our fair city's bins. The last time one checked, London wasn't exactly teeming with barns. If anyone is an immigrant, it is you, owl."

Hooter flapped his wings, but couldn't get off the branch he had been unceremoniously glued to almost three years ago. "Let me at him! Let me at him, the ginger scrotum!"

"This is not going to revenge creator," Vladimir said, riding all the way along the shelf and back again.

"Are we doing this minute's silence, or not?" Jemima quacked.

"Not," Jessica said.

Hooter settled once again upon his branch, though stared at Fairfax the Fox with a look that could kill. It was the glass eyes, you see. Nothing more menacing than a glass eye, which was probably why Columbo always caught his man.

"May one suggest," Fairfax said, "that in order to successfully avenge our creator, we, as a collective assemblage of mixed fauna, must fathom a way in which to throw off our respective restraints?"

"What?" said Hooter, frowning. "Speak English, fox, or heaven help me I'll set you on fire."

"What the fox is trying to say," said Bill, "is that if we're going to kill the bastards who did this, then we'd stand more of a chance if we weren't nailed or glued to pieces of wood."

"Precisely," Fairfax said, suavely raising an eyebrow, which was no mean feat, considering that just yesterday he was hanging up in an airing cupboard.

"And how are we supposed to free ourselves?" Hooter said. It was a damn good question—the kind of question one would expect from an owl. "Buffalo Bill is just a head, and Gerry's hooves have been glued to that mahogany mount for as long as I've known him."

"Actually," Gerry said, stepping off the mahogany mount. "The glue wore off years ago. I just didn't want to say anything, just in case it made you lot jealous." He did a little dance, tapping his cloven hoofs on the carpet like a long-necked version of Michael Flatley.

"So the giraffe is free," smiled the fox. "This is a good start, one thinks. And since one's glue is new, one shouldn't have too much difficulty…" He heaved, tugged and pulled on his legs, could feel the hard epoxy holding his paw in place. "…One almost… has it…" A hind leg broke free, and then the other, but now Fairfax was in a perpetual handstand, his two front legs still fixed to the board.

"Go on, foxy!" Buffalo Bill said. "You can do it!"

Fairfax dropped down and began kicking at his own front legs with his own back legs. "Sonofaspiffinggun!" he said. "This stuff holds well, doesn't it?"

"Hang on, Fairfax," Vladimir said. He slowly pedalled backwards, giving himself the best run-up possible on such a short shelf. "I know where creator keeps knives. I free you." The rat took a deep breath, and then pedalled as fast as he could toward the edge of the shelf, his tiny legs moving so quickly they became a furry blur.

And then the unicycling rodent was flying through the air, screaming, cursing his own stupidity, for he hadn't quite figured out how he was going to land. In a heap or on his head.

The other animals watched. They didn't have much choice, since their eyes were made of glass and their eyelids were glued open. It was like that scene in *A Clockwork Orange*, only instead of a TV screen filled with war and death, there was a Russian rat on a unicycle, screaming at the top of his lungs as he hurtled through the air toward almost certain death.

Surprisingly, the rat nailed the landing. And if he hadn't been busy celebrating the fact, he probably would have seen the wall coming at him at breakneck speed. Vladimir hit the wall with such force that the recently orgasmed man three miles away felt a slight tingle in his loins, put it down to wind and moved on with his life.

"I'm okay," Vladimir said, pushing himself up onto his wheel. "Everyone relax, Vlad is okay."

Hooter rolled his glass eyes. "Can we just get a wriggle on?" he said. "I'm pretty sure that at some point the police are going to show up, and we all know what they're like. Shoot first, ask questions later. And those questions will be: *Why the fuck were those stuffed animals all moving around as if they were still alive?* and *Why was that stupid fox wearing a tartan waistcoat and a monocle?"*

Fairfax had managed to pull his third leg free, and was now working on the final one. "Keep talking, barn owl," he said, breathless. "At least one isn't named after a tacky sports bar and grill chain in the US of A."

"Do you see an 'S' at the end of Hooter?" Hooter said. "No, because it ain't pissing there, you ginger twat—"

"Really not time for this," Vladimir said. He was circling the counter, looking for a way to reach Fairfax. "Really didn't think this through."

"Never mind the fox," said Jemima/Jessica. "We're stuck solid to this mount."

Gerry stopped dancing and clopped toward the two-headed duck. "I've got it," he said. "If I just…" He trailed off, extended his neck as far as it would go, and nudged Jemima/Jessica to the edge of the sill.

"No!" Jessica quacked.

"Definitely not!" added Jemima.

But it was far too late as Gerry poked them over the edge and they dropped to the floor, quacking and screaming and cursing the baby giraffe for being so heavy-handed. As they impacted—Jemima took the brunt of it—the wooden mount separated, and the two-headed duck bounced once, then twice, before landing on its side.

"Way to go, Gerry," Buffalo Bill said.

Gerry did a little jig, clearly pleased with himself.

"Don't praise the giraffe," Jemima/Jessica said, using

a wing to push herself onto her feet. "Could have killed us, the long-necked freak."

"One is free!" Fairfax said. The fox had managed to unstick its fourth and final leg, and was now stretching and licking the dried glue from its paws, despite not being able to generate any spittle.

"Me next," Hooter said. "I've been sitting on this branch since Obama was stabbing people in the ghetto."

"Your racism is terrible," Jemima/Jessica said, flapping frantically, relearning how to fly. "Do you think you should tone it down a bit?"

"Probably," Hooter said as the two-headed duck alighted upon the edge of the display cabinet in front of him. "I don't suppose either of you have access to a glass-cutter, do you? One of those things cat-burglars use to slice perfect circles in windows?"

"Hang on a minute," Jemima said, patting at her body with a wing as if checking pockets which weren't there. "No, I appear to have left my cat-burglar glass-cutter at home."

"Ooooh, sarcasm," Fairfax said, leaping down from the counter and, on still-stiff limbs, making his way across the room to where the owl sat in its glass display. "One likes that. One likes that a lot."

"Does everything have to be 'one' with you?" Hooter said. "What's wrong with 'I'?"

"One was brought up, not dragged up," Fairfax said. "For a creature whose diet subsists of mainly its own shit, you're awfully uppity." Hooter turned his attention back to the two-headed duck, which was pecking frantically at the glass. "And what is that going to achieve, exactly?" he said. "Are you trying to blunt your bills?"

"Fine," Jemima/Jessica said. "Stay in there. See if we care."

"One has an idea!" Fairfax said, circling the cabinet. "This thing is on castors. One calculates that a forward trajectory at just over thirty mph, resulting in a collision with the south wall, would be enough to free Hooters from his glass prison."

"It's *Hooter*," Hooter said. "Not *Hooters*. Now you're just being a dick."

"Why don't you just ask Gerry to knock the display over?" Buffalo Bill suggested.

"One hadn't thought of that," Fairfax said, checking his pocket-watch for no other reason than it made him look terribly refined. "Go ahead, Gerry. Smash that blighted thing to smithereens."

The giraffe danced across the room, neck popping from side to side as if moving to inaudible hip-hop—something by P-Diddy, perhaps, or Jay Zed. "Okay, everyone stand back," said Gerry. "I'm going to have to take a run at this one."

Inside the glass, Hooter squirmed nervously. "I'm not sure this is such a great idea," he said.

"It's a *spiffing* idea!" Fairfax said, moving away from the glass display. "Buckle up, Hootster, one is about to experience a little turbulence."

"I just don't think…" He trailed off as the baby giraffe pelted hell for leather toward his display. Four spindly legs tripped over one another as Gerry came to grips with gravity once again, and as he ran, his neck moved around in big circles. Unable to close his eyes, Hooter turned his head around to face the wall and braced for impact.

"Geronimo!" yelled Gerry as all four legs left the floor, the front two stretched out in front to toppled the display cabinet from its stand. Unfortunately, things didn't quite turn out the way Gerry had planned. The glass display, it turns out, was bolted to the cabinet beneath it, which meant that it wouldn't have budged even if you'd packed the display with dynamite and lit the fuse. As a result, the giraffe's front hooves went straight through the glass, knocking Hooter from his perch.

"Huuuuuuuuuuuuuuuurrrrrrrr," Hooter said, clearly winded.

"I think the display is bolted to the cabinet," Jemima/Jessica said. "That's probably why that didn't go to plan."

"Hurrrrrr," Hooter replied, dragging himself across the bottom of the display, a crippled mess, already considering the possibility of life on disability benefit.

"Well," said the debonair fox, "one can only applaud the efforts and bravery of Gerald. Thanks to him, the owl is free. Making some terrible noises and crawling like a drunken snail, but free."

Gerry retracted his front legs from the shattered display, apologising profusely to the injured barn owl who, credit where it was due, had already added two more sounds to his recovery. *Guh* and *Hooooooo*. The latter was perhaps the most important if you were an owl.

"Okay, so *now* what do we do?" Vladimir said, unicycling over the body of their dead creator, stopping when he arrived at Ted Barker's still chest. "Are we sure he dead? This will be embarrassing if he come back now."

"One isn't a doctor," Fairfax said, "but when a man loses half of his head and most of his face trying to stop a speeding bullet, one can safely assume he's reached the end of his life."

Hooter, pulling himself from the debris and out onto the shop floor, said, "He's dead. We saw those badfellas whack him off—"

"Wow!" Jemima/Jessica said. "I didn't think any of us would be sad enough to use the 'badfellas' joke."

"It was there for the taking," Hooter said. "Pretty good joke, if you ask me."

"Terrible joke," Vladimir said as he unicycled up toward what remained of Ted Barker's mouth. "When master is buried, pretty sure he will turn in grave at terrible joke."

"Pretty sure I'm not going to take joke advice from someone whose president is Putin," Hooter said.

"And—" But that was where he stopped talking as, off in the distance, sirens dopplered through the streets of London, drawing ever closer. Everyone fell silent, exchanged glances of trepidation. Fairfax the Fox inspected his pocket-watch once again; if only he had opposable thumbs, he could wind it up.

And the wail of the sirens grew louder and louder.

"We should probably—"

"Yeah, we should," Hooter said, interrupting Vladimir. "Out the back door, quick as you like!"

The stuffed animals rushed for the rear entrance. Feathers flew, fur was ruffled, and the thump of hooves upon carpet gave an old man three miles away the sudden urge to hit a nightclub.

BARKER'S STUFFED EMPORIUM (we take roadkill, but no hedgehogs!) was empty, save for the dead man lying upon its floor. And as the sirens drew closer, the camera which wasn't there panned up to reveal a sad buffalo head hanging upon the wall, staring nervously around.

"Guys?" Bill said, hoping they hadn't really forgotten him, that this was just some sort of sick ruse—a taxidermy trick. But a minute passed, and then another, and car doors were slamming shut out front and sirens were switched off. The crackle of approaching two-way radios could be heard.

Buffalo Bill put on his best play-dead face and hoped to God it worked.

7

Reginald Cline was having a bad day. Most days were bad—he was homeless, had been wearing the same underpants for three years, and seldom had anything to celebrate at the best of times—but this day was worse. He wished he hadn't rolled out of his cardboard box that morning. For today was the day he had finally been pushed too far.

Today was the day Reginald Cline self-diagnosed as being insane.

The day had started off much the same as always. He'd thought about brushing his teeth, realised he couldn't, and so instead swilled his mouth out with what remained of the previous night's cider—or battery-acid, as it was known amongst the homeless community. He'd then considered taking a shower, realised he didn't have one, and so quickly popped into the train-station toilet for a splash of water to his filthy face and a quick poo. All poos are quick if you are homeless; the lack of food and increase in liquids makes going to the toilet more of a game of chance rather than a thing of necessity. But this poo had been remarkably quick, so quick that he hadn't even needed to wipe afterwards.

Upon leaving the train station, Reginald had checked his schedule for the day—which had been scribbled on the back of an old bus-ticket with a stolen pencil from the bookies—and quickly came to the conclusion that the world was his oyster. "Reagh cha smaere bool," he had said in a language which only fellow homeless people understood. Roughly translated, he'd said: *Well, this is a turn-up for the books. I can do anything I please today, and what a fine day it is. No need for an umbrella today. My cardboard box will not be soggy when I crawl into it this eve. Why, I might even treat myself to a second poo later today.*

He had made his way back into town, preparing himself for a long day of sitting in front of an empty plastic cup, grunting at the passing public, when all of a sudden three men had rushed past him, almost knocking him from his feet, which were unsteady at the best of times.

"This fucking hobo!" one of the men had said. He reminded Reginald of Marlon Brando in that film with the sleeping fishes.

"You want me to whack him off, boss?" one of the men behind Brando had said, reaching for something concealed within his expensive-looking suit-jacket.

Now, Reginald Cline had not been whacked off in a very long time, at least not while he was awake to enjoy it, and so he thought he'd hit the lottery by this point, and began to nod frantically, wiping the drool from his beard and wondering what he had done to befall such good fortune.

The Brando one had leaned in and prodded Reginald in the chest with a strong finger. "You bump into me again, vagabond, and you'll be whacked off, capiche?"

Reginald had bumped into him again, hoping the offer still stood.

"What is this guy's fucking problem?" Brando had said.

"Think he's drunk, boss," one of the men at the rear had said. This one, Reginald saw, only had thumbs, which was something you didn't see every day, even if you were homeless.

Brando had grinned at Reginald. "Hey, drunken hobo, how much money do you make on an average day?"

Reginald had frowned. "Cler maas pertaki ak dyy mirake." Roughly translated: *I wouldn't get out of my box for any less than fifty pence per hour.*

The Brando one had pulled something from his pocket then—several sheets of folded paper. "Sign here, here, and here," he had said, and Reginald had signed here, here, and here because he was drunk and didn't know any better. Plus, he managed to smuggle the expensive-looking pen away when Brando had his back turned. "I'll collect at the end of every day. And remember, fifty percent of something is better than a hundred percent of fuck all." Whatever the hell that meant.

Reginald had nodded, waving the three nice gents away and wondering who they had mistaken him for that they should require, not one, but *three* autographs. *One for each of them, no doubt*, Reginald thought, and he did look a little like Brian Blessed—if Brian Blessed had become a raging alcoholic who ate the occasional packet of noodles and favoured shoe-polish over soap—so that must be it.

It was shortly after that strange run-in with Marlon Brando and his two friends that Reginald Cline's sanity became a thing of the past.

He slipped from the busy street into his alleyway—not really his alleyway, but the one in which he bedded down most nights due to its sought after location (three bins, regularly filled) and its lack of foot-traffic (you could pee anytime you wanted without fear of arrest or dismemberment). He was just about to create a roll-up cigarette out of eighty percent pocket-fluff, ten percent tobacco, and ten percent something else, when one of the large steel doors leading off the alleyway burst open and a fox, a baby giraffe, a two-headed duck, a racist-looking owl, and a rat on a unicycle came barrelling through it.

"What the…?" Reginald said, recoiling in horror.

"Out of the way, you dirty bastard!" the owl said, but it was too late. The owl was already smacking into his face. Reginald could taste its wings as they flapped about his face. He flailed around, mouth clenched shut so that the owl's willy didn't find a way in, and eventually he shook the creature off and turned to watch it, and the other animals, flee.

Then he heard sirens, nearby, and assumed they were here for him, for he was homeless and therefore constantly breaking the law, even when he wasn't trying. Perhaps it was an ambulance, arriving to cart him off to some sanatorium. It would be padded cells and nightly medication for Reginald from now on, or so he thought.

He collapsed into a heap next to his semi-detached cardboard box and began to sob, the taste of racist owl still on his tongue and thoughts of electroconvulsive therapy whirling through his soon-to-be labotomised brain.

*

On the next street sat a quaint coffee shop. The kind of place you could purchase a muffin and a latte and not see change from a twenty, *Java the Hut* was the go-to place for struggling writers and arsehole hipsters. In front of the café, cordoned off in order to make its customers feel like VIPs when in fact they simply had more money than sense, were a row of outdoor tables and chairs. And in one of those chairs sat a smoking woman.

Cynthia Berk had reached a personal-best level on Angry Turds, and was exceedingly pleased with herself. At forty, she was the perfect advertisement for why one should never take up Jobseeker's Allowance—or drugs, for that matter—but Cynthia Berk didn't care what people thought of her. To hell with them, and the horse they rode in on.

"Excuse me," a voice said, and a second later a timid barista stood before her. She knew he was a barista because of the large white wig and black gown.

Cynthia appraised the man's garb, and then said, "You're a barista. Why are you dressed as a barrister?"

"It's dress-up day," the barista said. "Look." He

motioned inside, beyond *Java the Hut*'s huge glazed frontage, to where a woman served an old man a cappuccino whilst decked out as a Nazi, while a second woman, wearing just a toga, wiped spilt milkshake from a recently-abandoned table.

"That's nice," Cynthia said, returning to level fifty-eight of Angry Turds. "Nice that you get to do fun things while you work."

"Yeah," said the barrister-barista. "You see, the thing is, you can't just sit out here if you're not drinking anything."

"I'm pretty sure I can," said Cynthia. "In fact, the fact that I'm doing it proves as much."

The barrister-barista looked perplexed for a moment, but Cynthia was too busy flinging poop to notice. "I know you *are* doing it," he eventually said, "but we have a policy, you see, which says that you shouldn't be doing it."

"Have a day off, mate," Cynthia said. "I'm not hurting anyone. I'm just resting my legs for a bit. Why don't you go back to your fancy-dress party and forget all about me?" She waved a hand dismissively through the air without taking her eyes off the mobile phone in her hand.

"Now, I've asked politely," said the barrister-barista, asserting himself the way he had been taught to do so on his training day, by throwing a leg up onto the awkward customer's table and tapping his foot. "You can sit there if you order a drink, that's fine, but otherwise I'm going to have no other choice but to—"

"Can I speak to your manager, please?" Cynthia paused her game, for this little sonofabitch was putting her off her stride.

"Excuse me?"

"Manager. I want to speak to your manager. The person in charge of this shit-show."

The barrister-barista removed his foot from the table and stared nervously back into the café. "Erm, my manager? She's not, erm, she's not in the best of moods this morning—"

"Are you going to fetch your manager, or do I have to walk in there and find her myself?" Cynthia was calling his bluff; she had no real desire to speak with anyone, let alone some coffee shop tart whose sole claim to fame was a Level 1 NVQ in food hygiene.

"*Giraffe!*" the barrister-barista suddenly blurted out. "*Giraffe, fox, two-headed duck!*"

For a second, Cynthia didn't know what was happening, but then she remembered a programme she had watched on Channel Four not so long ago—*Tourette's: Swearing Blind*—and realised what she was dealing with. "Oh! I'm so sorry! You're one of *them*, aren't you?" She straightened up in her seat, put the mobile phone down for the first time in three hours, and said, "*Cunt! Prick! Shitkebab!*" hoping it would put the poor man at ease.

"*Owl! Rat on a unicycle!*" the barrister-barista said.

"*Fanny! Michael Jackson's bedroom!*" Cynthia replied.

But the man was no longer paying her any attention whatsoever. Instead he was staring across the street, eyes wide, mouth agape, as if he had seen a ghost.

"What…" Cynthia turned just as a rat on a unicycle disappeared into a side-street. But that didn't make any sense to her, and so she chalked it up to too much lager last night. She pushed herself up from the chair and tucked her mobile phone away. "Well, I do hope you get those tics of yours sorted out," she said. "*Wanker!*" she yelled as she left the cordoned-off area and began to walk in the general direction of home. "*Arseburger! Toilet seat! Beyonce!*"

*

Martin Chuzzlechops sat in the barber's chair, staring at himself in the mirror, wondering how he had got to be so old. His eyebrows were silvering, his mouth was puckering, his teeth were yellowing; it was as if his whole head had just recently decided to give up and become a Geography teacher.

It was time to act, time to regain some of his youth before it was lost forever. A haircut was a good place to start; a reverse-vasectomy was definitely off the cards.

"Do you think you could do something… cool?" Martin said. "Something… something that will make me hip with the kids."

"I could Sellotape a picture of Kanye West over your face," said the barber, who was in the process of laying out all the instruments he required for this particular cut. "Might not go down too well in certain circles, but

76

it would certainly make for an interesting anecdote."

Martin shook his head. "No, I want something different this month, Geoff. Something that'll make me look *younger*."

Geoff the Barber sighed deeply and snipped the air once or twice with his scissors. "Having a bit of a mid-life crisis, Martin?" he said. "It comes to us all, you know. Nothing to worry about. Age is but a number, and you're only as old as the woman you feel, and things to that general nature."

"But the woman I'm feeling is ninety-two," Martin said, the bile rising in his throat as the previous night's intercourse with Ethel Gripe flooded his mind. "I'm forty-two, Geoff! I shouldn't be having sex with a nonagenarian."

"*Nobody* should!" said the barber. "Not even other nonagenarians." He stepped up behind his client and began running a comb through the thinning black hair sitting atop his head. "Have you ever considered a Mohawk? They're all the rage with the gangs in the city, and I reckon you've got just enough hair to pull it off."

Martin shook his head once again. Geoff wished he'd keep bloody still. "No, not a Mohawk," he said. "If I show up to work at the charity-shop with one of those, Ethel will have my guts for garters." He stroked his chin, stared at his phizzog in the mirror, and pondered what would actually look good on him.

"A reverse mullet?" Geoff said.

Martin frowned, and so did the face in the mirror,

the unoriginal bastard.

"It's like a mullet, only the long hair goes on the front of your face."

"I thought as much," Martin said. "But since I don't have a hairy face, I guess we'll have to come up with something else."

They both fell silent for a moment, and then another; all the time Geoff the Barber snipped noisily at the air, as if Claude Rains had popped in for a short back and sides.

"What about a… baby giraffe running across the street chased by various animals which shouldn't all be out during daylight hours?"

"Ooh, I like the sound of that," Martin said, smiling, intrigued. "Does it come with a free shave?"

"Out there!" Geoff said, shuffling across the shop toward the window. "There's a bloody baby giraffe out here pelting hell for leather down the High Street."

"Don't be daft," Martin said, climbing from the chair, which wasn't as easy as it sounded as it was one of those uppy-downy-spinny-roundy jobbies. "We don't have giraffes in this country. Unless it's escaped from the zoo."

"Take a look, if you don't believe me," Geoff said, stepping aside to allow his only customer a better view of the street.

"I'll be damned," Martin said. "That's a baby giraffe, Geoff! And it's being chased by… by an owl and a two-headed duck, and… is that a rat on a unicycle?"

"Of course it is!" Geoff said. "Russian as well, by the looks of him."

"Now *there's* something you don't see every day," Martin said, though it was something he had *never* seen before, and he'd had a lot of days, which was part of the reason why he was here, *at Scissor's Palace,* in the first place. "Probably filming something. This is London, after all. Maybe it's one of those, erm, those Disney films, the ones with the CGI characters and the morals and whatnot."

Geoff frowned. "You mean like the one with the toys that came to life. What was that one called. The story with the toys? The toy story… you know the one I mean…"

Martin nodded. "*Small Soldiers,*" he said. "Got it on video. *Great* film." And he moved across the room and retook his seat. Geoff pulled the sheet around his neck, and began to whistle tunelessly, snipping at the air and wondering what the hell he was going to do to make Martin look younger, short of major surgery.

A few minutes later, Martin said, "I didn't know that was how they made those films. I always thought they were built inside a computer. All graphics and stuff."

Geoff the Barber shrugged. "Don't suppose those lot would have fit inside a computer," he said, which might have been the most ridiculous sentence ever spoken in the history of London.

8

Gerry led the animals into a shadowy side street. He didn't think they had been spotted, but he was a taxidermy giraffe—had been ever since an African poacher got lucky seventy-five years ago—and so he was hardly an any position to assume anything.

"Oh, great!" Hooter said, landing atop a large industrial bin. "Are we going to be spending the rest of our lives running in and out of alleyways?"

"The giraffe take us to safety," said Vladimir, panting and wheezing and massaging his tiny rat thighs. He hadn't unicycled like that in many years. "We will not be seen here."

Fairfax loped from one end of the side street to the other, checking they weren't being followed. "One feels like one is about to suffer a coronary," he said. "Is that possible?"

The owl shook his head. "You're already dead, gingerbollocks. Plus, your heart's in a bin back at the shop. The worst you can expect from now on is dislodged stuffing or a warped polystyrene form. And believe me, that second one is a worse than it sounds."

"Hmmm," Fairfax said, standing up straight and dusting his waistcoat down. "One can see this is going to take a while to get used to."

"You really shouldn't be standing up like that," said Gerry, cantering from one side of the thin street to the other.

"Like what?"

"Like you're about to try to sell life insurance to a passer-by," Jemima/Jessica said. "If someone sees you, stood there like that, they'll either throw a net over you and escort you to the nearest Simon Cowell-fronted talent contest, or they'll throw a net over you and then beat you with a cricket bat. Either of those sound appealing?"

Fairfax dropped down onto all fours. "Not particularly," he said.

"And lose the shagging waistcoat," Hooter said. "You're a fox. You can get away with being a fox, just mooching around town, so long as you're not sporting something from Russ Abbott's wardrobe."

"Are you suggesting," Fairfax said, "that one removes one's waistcoat? That I, Fairfax, prowl around our fair city in a state of undress?"

"If you don't want to look like a complete dickhead," Hooter said, "then yes. That's exactly what I'm suggesting."

Fairfax pushed back up onto two legs and began dancing around, punching at thin air with clenched paws. "Then I must challenge you to a duel!" he said. "A fist-fight. Mano a mano. No pulling fur, and no plucking feathers."

"There really is no time for this," Vladimir said, steering himself around the shadow-boxing fox. "This isn't going to revenge master."

Ignoring the rat entirely, Hooter, wings extended,

floated down to the concrete and squared up to Fairfax. "Just who do you think you are?" he said, poking the fox with a firm wing. "You turn up like Paris Hilton, all fake-posh and full of shit, and expect us to take you seriously. Well, it ain't happening, Fuckface—"

"*Fairfax,*" the fox corrected.

"And I'll tell you another thing, you urban menace," said Hooter, poking Fairfax once again. "You don't belong with us. You're not one of us, and you don't have any reason to be with us."

Fairfax stood silent for a moment. Then, with a quivering bottom lip, he said, "It's because one is ginger, isn't it?"

"It's because you're a nobhead," Hooter said. "You're the Russell Brand of foxes. Do you even remember what life was like before… before that monocle was glued to your eye?"

The fox stared off into the distance. It was all very dramatic. "One does," he said. "One remembers it like it was yesterday."

*

The fox ran, and ran, and leapt over low fences, and ran some more, and behind him the men on horseback blew their horns and continued their chase. "This can't be happening!" the fox thought. "I've never done anything to hurt anyone. Why are they chasing me? Why are those barking dogs after me? What madness is this?"

Just an hour ago the fox had been doing foxy things, minding its own business, defecating in mole-hills and wondering which bin it was going to eat from later that evening. It had been fornicating with a rather splendid vixen when the first hunting horn sounded. The sudden noise had sent the vixen running for the hills, which had been a shame as the fox was so close to finishing.

Then, from out of seemingly nowhere, six men on horseback, wearing scarlet coats and black velvet caps, had come barrelling over the hill. At the feet of the horses, English foxhounds excitedly kept pace.

"Tally-ho!" the master of hounds had bellowed.

"Fuck the fuck off!" the fox had yelled back, before taking off as quickly as it possibly could in the direction of the vixen.

And now it was running, and those upper-class knobs with their Etonian educations kept on coming. It was a nightmare. Every fox's worst nightmare come true.

The fox could almost feel the hounds' breath upon his tail, could almost smell the excitement emanating from the chasing pack.

The horn sounded again. Da-daaa-da-daaa! It was a catchy tune, and one the fox would be humming for the rest of the day should it survive the next three minutes.

"Tally-ho!" the master of hounds repeated.

"Your mom's a ho!" the fox whined. Now, if the fox had known they would be its last words, it would have perhaps chosen more wisely, but the fox wasn't privy to such precognition, and so when the first hound latched onto its hind leg, it was far too late to come up with anything better.

The fox howled as the hound's jaws clamped down hard, and then it was rolling, barrelling across the grass with hounds snapping at its body, tearing chunks from it, and generally not playing fair.

The fox closed its eyes as the pain first worsened and then subsided, as sharp teeth ripped into it, and as the sound of posh knobs congratulating one another— "High-five, Rupert!"— slowly faded away.

*

"That is *terrible* story," Vladimir said, circling Fairfax's feet. "You should perhaps keep to yourself from now on. Very upsetting."

Hooter stepped away from the fox. He'd had no idea that Fairfax's death had been so brutal, and felt bad for bringing it up, but only for a moment. "You see?" he said. "You're not some posh git. You're just a fox… dressed up like a posh git. I'm pretty sure that if we remove that monocle from your eye, you will still be able to see."

Fairfax shrugged. "One guesses so," he said. "But—" And that was where the sentence ended as a sweeping brush slammed into Fairfax, knocking him across the side street. At the end of the brush stood an old woman. Cream cardigan, tissues balled up and wedged into sleeves, ill-fitting false teeth; she was the epitome of old lady. If you were to ask someone what they thought an old lady should look like, this woman would be what they described.

And yet she was swinging a sweeping brush like a champion samurai, trying to hit the animals gathered around her, and screaming in a forty-fags-a-day voice, "Devils! Devils in my back yard!"

Through blurred vision, Fairfax watched as Hooter leapt into the air, swooped back down upon the old lady, pecking at her liveried head and flapping frantically at her face in an attempt to render her unconscious.

"Where did mad lady come from?" Vladimir squeaked, steering around the old lady's cankles. "Why humans always they try to kill us?"

The old lady screamed. "A talking rat!" she gasped. "On a unicycle, of all things! Devil rat! Rat of the Devil!"

Jemima pecked at the old lady's foot while Jessica pecked at the other. The old lady glanced down and, upon seeing the two-headed duck, screeched, "Demonic ducks! Oh, Satan, how you taunt me with these evils!" She kicked out, sending Jemima/Jessica flying. The two-headed duck landed with a thump against a wooden door.

"Someone take this old bag down!" Jemima screeched.

"That's someone's grandma you're talking about!" Jessica reminded her fellow head.

"Ain't mine!" Jemima replied.

Gerry, who had been standing in shock at the side of the street deciding whether or not to get involved, suddenly bolted forwards. When the old lady saw the giraffe, she screamed once again, and this time she dropped the sweeping brush and it clattered to the ground. "Devil-giraffe! Long-necked demon from Africa!"

"That's a bit harsh," Gerry said, colliding with the old lady and sending her staggering backwards. For the longest time she seemed to balance precariously on her heels; in fact, so much time passed that Fairfax, his vision clearing, was able to check his pocket-watch several times. When the old lady finally went down, it was with a sickening thud and a groan of pain and despair.

She was unconscious, unmoving. Hooter cautiously approached the felled geriatric. "I think she's knocked herself out," he said. "Phew, she was a nasty one, wasn't she?"

"Where did she come from?" Gerry asked.

"One would hazard," Fairfax said, "that the old biddy came from over there." He pointed across the street to where a door stood open, though which various clothes were visible, hanging upon rails. "Looks like some sort of… some sort of charity shop."

"We need to get the body off the street," Hooter said, motioning to the old lady. "Probably only weighs fifty pounds wringing wet. Reckon we can drag her over there?"

Gerry and Fairfax arrived at the side of the old lady. "Should be able to," Gerry said, clamping onto the old lady's crotch with his mouth. Fairfax recoiled in horror, but then the baby giraffe was carrying the old lady toward the door all on his own, and so Fairfax—and the rest of the animals—decided not to question the giraffe's unsanitary methods.

Once inside, they lay the woman out in the middle of the shop, surrounded by objects of varying worthlessness, and made sure all the doors were locked.

"So now what do we do?" Jemima asked. "Those Mafiosos are getting away, and we're locked up in a charity shop with an unconscious old dear. Can any of you tell me how this is going to help us avenge our creator?"

Fairfax walked across the shop to where the cash register sat upon a white unit. He began to push the buttons upon the till, each button he pressed accompanied by a digital beep.

"What the hell are you up to, Fairfax?" Hooter said. "Are we really going to rob this poor woman? Don't you think knocking her out is enough for one day? I mean, she must be ninety-two years old. Yes, this woman is exactly ninety-two, and according to her name-badge, her name is Ethel. You really want to rob poor Ethel while she lies here, half dead, surrounded by all this worthless tat?"

"That was incredibly specific," Fairfax said. "If one didn't know better, one would suggest you were aggressively trying to reveal this woman's identity to further the plot of this story."

"Don't be absurd," said the barn owl, turning to wink at a camera that wasn't there.

Fairfax pushed a button upon the till and the drawer flew open, smashing him right in the monocle. "Done it!" he said. Then he was riffling through the drawer, sending banknotes and receipts flying across the room. He stopped to read one receipt, which was, it turned out, a return slip for a pair of ADIDAS tracksuit bottoms, ninety-five pence. "Who returns things to a charity shop?" he said. "I mean, one really does despair sometimes."

"Is there purpose for violating woman's business?" Vladimir asked, incredulous. "Hooter right. It bad enough we rattle her brain and cause her possible death, but Vlad feel like rummaging through old lady knicker drawer, and it not good feeling."

"I feel like we're missing someone," Hooter said.

"We're all here," said Jemima, glancing around and performing a cursory head-count.

"Got it!" Fairfax said, lifting the money tray from the till and removing a stapled document. "One has a clue to find those murderous bastards!" It was a contract, signed at the bottom by one Ethel Gripe, and confirming that half of the charity shop's profits would now be forwarded to Paparella's Protection Services (we whack people off, sometimes for fun!) Ltd.

"I'm certain there should be more of us," Hooter reiterated.

"Stop being silly, owl," Vladimir said. "We are all present and correct."

"There doesn't seem to be an address on this contract," Fairfax said. "Well, surely that's a red flag, right there."

"No address means it's useless to us," Jemima said.

"Might as well be holding a sign which says UP SHIT CREEK WITHOUT A PADDLE."

"There's definitely someone missing," Hooter said, wings on hips.

"Devil creatures!" the old lady squealed as she dragged herself back from consciousness and tried to push herself up onto bony elbows. "The power of Christ compels you! The power of Christ—"

A candlestick to the head—50p, and a bargain at that—silenced the crazed biddy, and she went down again. This time, however, she wasn't breathing.

Gerry the Giraffe dropped the candlestick and took a step away from the body. "I didn't... is she..."

"Yes, you clobbered lady to death," Vladimir said, checking Ethel Gripe's pulse. It was no longer there. "On bright side, she very old. When lady get to her age, she yearn for death."

"You did her a favour," Jemima quacked. "She's in a better place now, Gerry."

Gerry didn't buy it.

"Fuck!" Hooter said. "Bill!"

"Who?" Fairfax said.

"Buffalo Bill!" Hooter replied. "I knew we were missing someone. We left the bloody buffalo head hanging on the wall back at Barker's."

"Hmmmm," Fairfax said, stroking his chin. "One wonders how that is going."

9

Detective Inspector Grant Tyler arrived on scene a moment after the boys in blue had moved through it like a whirlwind. Any evidence they might have gathered was now surely destroyed, thanks to PC Ricks and his overweight colleagues, moving through the shop like drunken men on a stag-do jostling for position at the bar. DI Tyler would have been angry, had it not been his own fault for stopping off to pick up a box of doughnuts. Some stereotypes were simply true, which was why PC Ricks—a reckless and suicidal cop, mulleted, recently transferred due to his use of excessive force—had been partnered with PC Murtow—a middle-aged black guy with a wonderful family and less than three weeks to retirement. These things sometimes write themselves.

"Ricks! Murtow!" DI Tyler said, pushing his way through a sea of obese law-enforcers. "My office right now!"

Ricks and Murtow exchanged a suspicious glance as their superior headed into the back room of the shop. They followed. He was carrying what appeared to be a tray of doughnuts. Of *course* they bloody followed.

"Close the door," said DI Tyler as Ricks and Murtow came through it. Murtow did as he was told. He had respect for authority, unlike his partner, who saw his supervisors as a thing to be challenged, to be wound up to the point that they, too, were suicidal. Simply put,

Ricks was an arsehole. "What the hell happened here?" DI Tyler said, stuffing the first doughnut whole into his mouth. His next words were muffled and practically indecipherable. "Wethotathedthathithermitht outhere!"

Ricks leaned in closer. "We've got a dead… taxidermist… out there?"

DI Tyler nodded. "Whathayooathodamntharrot?"

"What are you, a goddamn carrot?" Ricks said, unsure what that even meant.

"Atharrotarthole—"

"A parrot, arsehole!" Murtow said, slapping his insubordinate partner across the mullet.

Fortunately, DI Tyler had finished the doughnut and was now pacing around the room, shaking his head and occasionally sighing. "We've got a murdered man, shot at close range in his own place of work. Now what does that tell you?" He turned to the 1980s buddy-cop duo and waited.

"I don't know about Murtow," Ricks said, "but it tells me that we've got a hitman on our hands."

Murtow sighed. "A hitman? I've got three weeks until I retire. The most we've ever had to deal with around here is serial dogging up on the Heath, and now we've got some badass sonofabitch going around, popping our taxidermists? I'm too old for this shit."

Ricks shrugged. "I'm a lunatic. Should probably be locked up before I kill someone, most likely myself but I'll take as many people with me when I go, because I'm selfish like that."

Murtow frowned.

"What?" Ricks said. "I thought we were sharing stuff?"

"Alright, arseholes," DI Tyler said. "We all know who did this. This is the work of Don Paparella and his crew. It's got 'mafia hit' written all over it. That poor schmuck out there probably refused to sign over half his takings, and Paparella whacked him off."

Ricks snorted. He was immature like that. Murtow kicked Ricks in the shin. He was the sensible of the two, and if Ricks wanted an invite to the Murtow Family Christmas this year—so that he could flirt with Murtow's daughter, who was terrible at beat-boxing— he would show the detective-inspector some goddamn respect.

"So what are we going to do about it?" Murtow said. "We sure as hell can't let murder go unpunished. Not in this town. Not on my watch."

"That's exactly what we're going to do," DI Tyler said. "You want us to go up against the mafia, Murtow? Is that what you're suggesting we do?"

"Those fanny-farts aren't *mafia*," Ricks said. "They come from Brentford and speak Cockanese when no one's looking. I'm pretty sure the one with only thumbs for hands plays dominoes at my local pub. Struggles to open a packet of pork scratchings, that one."

DI Tyler angrily straightened. "They're the closest thing we've got to mafia in this country," he said. "And those guns they're carrying sure ain't water-pistols.

Don't believe me? Ask the guy with half his face missing lying on the floor out there." He pointed toward the door. "Oh, you can't. Because half his face is missing. Do you know of any water-pistol that could do that kind of damage?"

Ricks nodded. "The Supersoaker 5000," he said. "Been known to melt the faces of children clean off…"

Murtow kicked him in the shin once again. Ricks's mullet wavered atop his head.

"We ain't gonna do a damn thing about this," DI Tyler said. "If I hear either of you are on this case, I'll bust you down to traffic duty. You hear me?"

Murtow nodded.

Ricks said, "We don't have traffic duty in this country. That's what traffic wardens are for."

Murtow hit his partner with a dead-arm.

"Then I'll make sure you spend the rest of your short career on the force behind a desk. Filling in Excel spreadsheets. And you won't have access to Solitaire. Or Minesweeper."

"I'm too old for this shit," Murtow groaned.

"Can I have one of those doughnuts?" Ricks said, motioning to the open box in front of the detective-inspector.

DI Tyler glanced down at the box, then at Ricks, then at Murtow who was shaking his head and muttering something about having only three weeks to go. "You can have one of the jam ones. But not one of the jam and custard ones. They're my favourite."

Upon leaving the back room, Murtow turned to his maverick partner, whose face was smeared with jam and custard. Once again, Ricks had decided that fire was a great toy, there to be played with. "So I guess we're just going to ignore this murder," he said, stepping over the corpse taking up most of the floor. "Want to go hang around the skate park? Bust a couple of kids for illegal trickery?"

Ricks wiped his mouth with the back of his hand. "We can't just ignore this, Murtow," he said. "Those pricks are out there with guns—or Supersoaker 5000's—and they're taking down good people. People like Ted Barker, whose only crime in life was giving animals a second chance."

"But the detective—"

"Tyler's in on it!" Ricks said in what turned out to be a shout-whisper. "Don't you see? The whole force is scared of Paparella. I heard the chief-superintendent signed one of those contracts himself, which is why we've now got to pay for our own handcuffs. Why we've got to share our toilets with the guys from the cricket club. Why your pension's been slashed in half."

"I can't get involved with this, Ricks. I've got three weeks to go until I—wait a damn minute. Did you just say my pension's been slashed in half?"

"Right down the middle, Murtow," Ricks said. "Paparella's going to be living it up on precisely half of your pension. Think about it. All those years on the force to make sure that sonofabitch can order lobster instead of beans on toast."

"We've got to do something, Ricks!" Murtow said, more animated than he had been in twenty years. "Tash finds out about this, I'll be divorced by the end of the week."

"That's not going to happen, Murtow," Ricks said, pulling his truncheon out. "We're going to bring Paparella down and put an end to all this madness."

Murtow sighed. "I'm too old for this shit."

*

Buffalo Bill stared down at the 1980s buddy-cop duo, listening to their clichéd conversation and trying to figure out whether this was the first in a new franchise or an unnecessary sequel. They hadn't noticed him, hanging up there on the wall, but apparently he was invisible, even to his friends who had pissed off without him. Bill figured he was probably best out of it. Let them all go off and get themselves re-killed, if that were even possible. Bill would probably end up in some paedophile's attic or hanging in a going-out-of-business public house for all eternity, and that was okay with him. He knew his place, and his place was not hunting down a trio of fake Mafiosos in order to exact revenge. Then again, whose was?

As he listened, Bill became aware that this stereotypical duo was going to take the case on, despite the warning from their superior. *Such a cliché*, Bill thought. At the end of all this, with Paparella and his boys in jail, or better, bludgeoned to death with truncheons, the detective-inspector would inevitably promote this unlikely pairing, make them detectives, and tell them that they had done the right thing by pursuing the case when all around people told them not to.

That was how this worked. Bill knew because he had spent a large part of his life hanging in Bruce Willis's bathroom.

"Hang on a minute!" the black cop said, suddenly squaring up to Bill. "I could have sworn I just saw this head mouth something."

"*Mouth* something?" the white cop with the mullet replied. "Buffalo heads don't mouth things. You're thinking of Pamela Anderson. Pamela Anderson mouths things."

The black cop stepped back, eyeing Bill with no small amount of suspicion. "Looked like it mouthed the words 'Bruce Willis'."

The white cop with the mullet frowned. "Buffalo heads don't mouth 'Bruce Willis', Murtow," he said. "You're getting too old for this shit."

"I am," the black cop said, turning away from Bill. "I am getting too old for this shit. Come on, let's go get something to eat, figure out what we're going to do next."

As they went—the black one mumbling something or other about having three weeks to go and the white one with the mullet slipping into a straitjacket and taking bets from those present—Bill heaved a sigh of relief.

That had been close.

Too close.

Fucking Bruce Willis, Bill thought.

10

The afternoon went by in a flurry. The dead animals walked around the charity shop discussing tactics, how they were going to locate Don Paparella, and what they would do to him when they did. Gerry suggested torture, to begin with, followed by a long and painful death, perhaps the removal of limbs followed by a disembowelment, culminating in an acid bath.

For a baby giraffe, he was one sadistic sonofabitch.

Fairfax, on the other hand, favoured a more quintessentially British method of torture. "One could force him to watch the entire run of *Downton Abbey*," he had suggested. "We could pin his eyes open, and force him to drink Earl Grey without any sugar. We could force-feed him cucumber sandwiches until he darn well apologises for his behaviour." And while there was something moderately evil about the fox's approach, the other taxidermy decided it didn't quite befit the crime. "Shame," Fairfax had said. "One missed the last three episodes."

As the sun disappeared behind the buildings opposite, casting the shop in semi-darkness—not the ideal shade of gloom when there is a creepy old lady lying dead on the floor—and turning simple items of furniture and clothes rails into shadowy hellish creatures from another world, the taxidermy gathered behind a tattered chaise longue to settle upon a course of action.

"Okay," Hooter said. "It's getting dark out there, which obviously suits me just fine, being a barn owl and whatnot. Clearly we can't stay here all night. Well, I guess we could, but that would mean spending more time in the company of that geriatric zombie over there, and she's already starting to kick up a bit of a pong, so I put it to you that our trail of vengeance begins this very night." He folded his wings across his chest, seemingly pleased with his opening speech.

"Are we going to go back for Bill?" Jemima said.

"And what use is Bill to us?" Gerry replied. "He's a head. The head of a water buffalo. He's less useful than tits on a fish."

"We could always throw him at the baddies," Jessica suggested. "Use him as sort of a furry grenade, only instead of exploding he'd probably just complain."

"We're not using Bill as a furry grenade," Hooter said, shuffling papers for no other reason than it looked good, and that people in meetings, such as this one, always shuffled papers. "There is no way we can return to the shop. The police will be all over that place like pre-pubescent teens at a Westlife concert. Bill's just going to have to tough it out alone for a few days, until we get this sorted, until we take down the Brentford

Mafia with our own brand of Furry Vengeance."

"I don't think we can say that," Gerry sniffed.

"Say what?" Hooter asked. "Furry—"

"Ah, ah, ah," said the giraffe. "We might be able to get away with it once, but say it twice and we'll have Brendan Fraser's lawyers all over us."

Hooter frowned and shook his head. "I have no idea what you're talking about, you lanky carpet-pattern, so I'm just going to continue. Is that okay with you?"

Gerry nodded. *Fine by me. Crack on, Hedwig.*

"Bill's a big boy, older than some of us combined." Hooter's head twisted unnaturally left and right as he spoke, taking in all those present, and making them all a little uncomfortable. "He can be our fly-on-the-wall, so to speak. Reckon he'll be taking in everything those cops are saying right about now—"

*

"I spy with my little eye, something beginning with… D." Bill mumbled, staring down on the corpse of Ted Barker, now lying in an unzipped body-bag. "Is it dead body?" he asked himself. "Yes. Yes, it is." The answer had been the same for the past two hours. "I spy, with my little eye, something beginning with… D." Fuck, he was bored.

*

"—and that information might be important to us later on." Hooter scratched his tummy. "If we're going to stand any chance of finding those murderous bastards and taking them down, we need eyes and ears everywhere, and Bill is perfectly placed to glean information from the cops—"

*

Bill listened to the policemen as they chatted just a few feet in front of him. Apparently, according to a young-looking PC whose face looked as if it had been unceremoniously stretched in order to house all its features, Aston Villa had just been relegated from the Premier League, and according to a feline-looking WPC, Michael Jackson wasn't a filthy paedophile! No, he wasn't! He just liked kids, that's all! He just liked kids!

Bill made a mental note of these two things, just in case the other animals ever returned.

*

"—so I think we can all agree that leaving Buffalo Bill there is a good idea." Hooter searched the faces of those surrounding him, looking for any sign of dissent.

Fairfax, who had been licking his own anus for the past five minutes, stopped momentarily to say, "One might have an idea. It is just an idea, so don't shoot one down—"

"What is it, gingerbollocks?" Hooter said.

"Yes," Vladimir added, teetering back and forth upon his tiny unicycle. "What is idea, Fairfax? We don't have all night."

Fairfax smiled. His whiskers twitched and his monocle almost disappeared wholly into the fox's crow's feet. "One has, in one's hand, a signed contract from Paparella's Protections Services (*fuck the police, fuck,*

fuck, fuck the police!) Ltd."

"We can see that," Jemima said. "You've been clutching the thing ever since you found it in the till."

"And although there is no business address upon said document," Fairfax said, "there is, of course, a payment schedule, a day upon which this establishment should expect a visit from messrs Paparella, Gambone, and Arminio. A collection itinerary, so to speak."

"Are you suggesting that we stay here, in this place with that dead old lady rotting in the corner, until next Friday?" Hooter said, incredulously. "She'll be a puddle by then. We'll have to mop her up. They'll smell her as soon as they set foot through that door. Shit, I can smell her already—"

"I agree," said Fairfax, "that the aforementioned corpse lying but a few feet away would be wholly disgusting in a week's time. However, according to this contract, the man calling himself Don Paparella—whose real name is probably Jim or Dave—is, in fact, to return to this very charity shop in the morning." The fox grinned.

"That would make sense," opined Vladimir. "Saturday mornings are best time for charity shop. Might as well shut rest of week."

Hooter, for the first time that night—the first time since he had flown into a double-glazed window, then proceeded to slide down it until he was nothing but a crumpled tangle of feathers and death on the patio— also grinned. "We don't even have to leave this place," he said. "They're coming to us. Furry Vengeance will be ours!" He laughed manically, hooting in between guffaws, and pretty soon they were all laughing, all making fools of themselves, all praising the taxidermy gods for such good fortune.

Their laughter was broken by the shrill ring of an old-fashioned telephone.

"Who could that be?" Hooter asked, face awash with puzzlement.

Fairfax leapt up onto the sales unit, to where the telephone sat ringing. He snatched the handset from its cradle and said, "Hello?" The tinny and distant voice of the person on the other end of the line trickled from the speaker, and when it was finished, Fairfax said. "We apologise profusely, sir. It will not happen again." He slowly placed the handset back onto its cradle and, to the nervous taxidermy, said, "Yes, that was the lawyer of one Mister Brendan Fraser. We are to cease and desist any further use of the term 'Furry Vengeance', lest we seek to incur serious charges and possible jail time."

<h2 style="text-align:center">11</h2>

When Ricks and Murtow walked into The Swan with Three Tits, all illegal activity ceased instantly. A serious poker game over in the far corner became nothing more than a friendly spot of Bridge. The old witch, Caroline Munster, stopped hawking illegal tobacco products and settled into a chair, a beatific smile spread across her face as if butter wouldn't melt. Word of the constables' arrival had reached three sets of homosexuals in the men's toilets, and they all came out with their tails between their legs—at least, they *looked* like tails—and tried to act as if they hadn't, just a moment ago, been partaking in a little buggery. Behind the bar, Jasper Quim was surreptitiously rearranging bottles, so that the imported stuff was at the back and your regular fare was at the front. At the end of the bar, two prostitutes closed their legs and put away their diaries. Unfortunately, nothing could be done about the illegal display that was Martin Chuzzlechops's new haircut.

"Ricks and Murtow!" Jasper said as the policemen arrived at the bar. "Off-duty, are we?"

Ricks nodded, removed his mullet and set it down next to the pubic-hair peanuts. "Double scotch, Quimmy, if you don't mind," he said. "I'm feeling particularly reckless tonight. Might even go and track me down some South African diplomats, start a fight, you know how it goes."

"I'm too old for this shit," said Murtow, plonking himself down on a stool next to Ricks.

"A pint of the black stuff for my friend here," Ricks added. "And by that I mean Guinness, not treacle."

"Right you are," Jasper said, and off he went to prepare drinks.

"Why are we here?" Murtow said. "I should be at home with my wife and kids, Ricks. You know I don't drink. Tash smells Guinness on my breath, I'll be divorced by the end of the week."

"She's really got you under the thumb, hasn't she?" Ricks said, smiling and putting his mullet back on. "You're undercover, Murtow. And being undercover means you have to do things you wouldn't otherwise do."

"I wouldn't otherwise drink Guinness, Ricks," Murtow said. "Hate the stuff."

"*No one* likes Guinness," Ricks said. "Not even the Irish, but your undercover persona will drink a pint of it, now and then, just to show he doesn't have a problem with the Irish. That's how it works, Murtow. You're a *great* undercover cop."

"Here you go," said Jasper Quim, placing a double scotch and a pint of Guinness down on the counter. "So what brings you two in here? Shouldn't you be out chasing bad guys? Escorting suicidal people down from the tops of buildings in the only way Ricks knows how?"

"We're undercover," Ricks said, sipping furtively at his scotch. "Don't tell anyone."

"Undercover, are we?" Jasper said, trying to sound enthused. "Wow. Isn't that what the detectives usually do? I mean, no disrespect to you guys—you do a great job of beating up smack-heads and arresting horny husbands for kerb-crawling—but isn't undercover work a little above your pay-grade?"

"That's what I said," said Murtow.

"Funnily enough, that's what DI Tyler said, too," added Ricks. "But I'm unhinged, liable to kill myself and then kill all of you straight after. You can't predict what I'm going to do next." He sunk his hand into the pubic-hair peanuts and tossed them into his mouth. "See? No one in their right mind would do something that crazy." He began beating himself around the head. "I'm a lunatic! He's the sensible one!" He pointed at Murtow, who was trying to make himself as small as possible.

"Take it down a notch, Ricks," Murtow said, dribbling Guinness back into the glass he'd just sipped it from. "We're undercover, remember?"

Ricks settled. "God, I wish Patsy Kensit was here right now," he said. "Anyway, we're looking for information on Don Paparella. We believe he's connected to the murder of Ted Barker, a local taxidermist."

Jasper recoiled in horror for dramatic effect. "Ted Barker's dead?" he gasped. "Oh my! That can't be right. He was in here just last night kicking up a fuss. I'm sure you're mistaken."

"Saw the body ourselves," Murtow said. "Half of his face had been shot off. If we're mistaken, the poor sonofabitch is going to spend the rest of his life drinking through a straw and avoiding mirrors."

The landlord's mouth fell wide open. The few teeth he had were discoloured, like rotten tombstones. It was a mouth which hadn't seen a dentist since the death of

Princess Diana, though the two events were not intrinsically connected. "If Barker's dead, I feel sorry for the poor bugger set to inherit those ghastly animals of his. Especially that two-headed duck thingamajig."

Ricks frowned, and so did his mullet. "What two-headed duck thingamajig?" he said. And then added, "That was a sentence I never thought I would use."

Jasper, now cleaning a glass with what appeared to be a pair of old lady pants, said, "That abortion he keeps in his shop. Ugly little quacker. Two-headed duck, but I don't think it's genuine. I mean, when was the last time either of you saw a two-headed duck knocking about the place?"

Ricks and Murtow shrugged.

"Yeah, I reckon it was something he put together himself in an attempt to appeal to those fascinated by the morbid, the macabre, the plain wrong." He placed the now-dirty glass down on the shelf behind him and took down a clean one, which he proceeded to scrub.

"But there wasn't a two-headed duck at the scene of the crime," Murtow said.

"Of course there bloody well was," replied the landlord. "It's been there since he took over the place. Can't sell it. There's no call for two-headed ducks in Chiswick."

"We definitely would have remembered a two-headed duck," Ricks said. "We're policemen. It's our job to be in tune with our surroundings at all times."

Over in the corner, the poker game was secretly back

in motion, and the two prostitutes at the end of the bar had serviced three punters under the counter.

"In that case," Jasper said, "the old fool must have moved it, but I'll bet it's there somewhere. Next to the baby giraffe, perhaps, or underneath the shelf upon which sits a Russian rat riding a unicycle."

Ricks and Murtow exchanged confused glances. Inside Murtow's head, a voice said *You're too old for this shit.*

"None of those things were there," Ricks said, knocking back his scotch. "And how do you know the rat is Russian?"

"Because Barker says it is," Jasper said. "But… I don't understand. Those pieces of taxidermy have been there since forever. Who in their right mind would shoot the old man in the face and then steal a bunch of ugly stuffed creatures?"

Ricks gestured to his empty glass, and Jasper Quim refilled it. "Unless Don Paparella has a penchant for deceased ornamental animals," he said, "I'm at a loss."

The landlord scratched his balding head. "You think this is the work of the Brentford Mafia?"

"We *know* it is," Murtow said. "That's why we're undercover. The DI finds out we're investigating Don Paparella and his cronies, we're going to be busted down to traffic duty."

"Lucky for you we don't have that in this country," Jasper said. "That's what traffic wardens are for."

Ricks turned and scanned the bar for illegal activity.

There was a card game taking place across the room; money was exchanging hands. Not necessarily a criminal offence. Perhaps they were just mates, handing back the tenners they had borrowed from one another. At the end of the bar, two ageing women—whose make-up appeared to have been applied by a leaf-blower—were being chatted up by a young man. The young man was grunting and sweating a little as one of the cougars licked at his earlobe. It was nice, Ricks thought, that even after a certain age, women could still enjoy themselves.

"Do you have a napkin?" the young man said to the landlord, turning on his stool. "I appear to have made a little mess." The ageing women giggled at that; Ricks giggled along with them, though he hadn't a clue why.

"How do you keep this place so above board?" Ricks asked Jasper.

The landlord shrugged nervously. "So, what are you going to do about Paparella?" he said, quickly changing the subject. "He's taking over the whole town, bit by bit. Pretty soon he'll be too powerful to stop. Might even make it all the way to the top. I'm talking mayor here."

"Since we're not officially on the case," Murtow said, winking conspiratorially in the direction of the landlord, who smiled and winked back, for no other reason than it seemed rude not to, "we're not obliged to divulge any details right now—"

"In other words, we haven't a fucking clue," Ricks said. "But there's something fairly odd about those missing animals. It's really playing on my mind now. Has been ever since you told us about them a minute ago."

"Like I said," said Jasper, "unless he's moved them, put them in storage, they've been half-inched by someone. What other explanation could there be. The dead animals came to life and walked out of there of their own volition?" He laughed manically.

Ricks laughed hard, too.

And Murtow.

They all laughed together for the longest time.

"Good one!" Ricks said, wiping the tears from his eyes.

"Dead animals… came to life!" Murtow sniggered. "I'm… too old… for this shit!"

"Another drink, fellas?" Jasper said. It was, he had learned over the years, best to get the punters while they were in a good mood, and his joke had seemingly gone down so well that he reckoned he could get at least another score out of the mulleted one.

"Go on then," Ricks said, sliding his glass across the counter. "One more, and then we're off. We've got a case to investigate, starting with that shop and those missing animals."

"We going back to the scene of the crime?" Murtow asked.

"That's where the clues will be," Ricks said, slipping into his straitjacket and turning to face the rest of the pub. "Step right up!" he said, dislocating his shoulder in preparation. "Thirty seconds or less, or your money back!"

12

The dancing girl was so close to Don Paparella's face that he could smell what she had had for breakfast. Something with kippers, apparently, and although he liked the girl—Debbie Faultner, 19, huge student debts she would never pay off and a lovely pair of eyes, if you liked that sort of thing—he wasn't in the mood for such close quarters tonight.

"Take a break, Debbie," he said, shouting over the thumping music which trickled from the speakers at the back of the stage. "And maybe a shower."

The girl, apparently hurt by the words of her employer, stormed off in the direction of the curtains—£18.99, Argos, Item Number 237-411—and disappeared, leaving only a faint whiff to suggest she had ever been there at all.

The club, GANGSTER'S PARADISE, was quiet tonight. Paparella scoured the room, saw the regulars doing their normal thing. Leaning against the bar there was Jimmy the Shit. Jimmy was a good guy, trustworthy despite his name—which had been given to him by Paparella on account that Jimmy suffered terribly with IBS. In that moment, Jimmy was chatting to Sindy, with an 'S' because spelling it with a 'C' was simply not slutty enough. Sindy had worked at GANGSTER'S PARADISE for as long as the place had been open, and she was a good girl, if not a little goofy. It was almost as if she had been given the teeth of two people—and maybe a horse—but apart from that she was a stunner. Occasionally, Paparella liked to play those teeth like a glockenspiel. He was rude like that.

On the other side of the room, sitting around a large oval table, were the rest of the likely lads. Vincenzo 'The Snout' Carmichael—whose moniker came from the fact he had a massive red nose—sat reading a newspaper, stopping to circle a horse every now and then with a stolen pencil—Argos once again, and completely free if you've got the balls to help yourself.

Next to Vincenzo, and sipping blackcurrant Fruit Shoot through a straw, was Thumbs, and next to Thumbs was Baby-Teeth. They were playing *Guess Who?* and neither of them was winning.

A little closer to the stage, Michael 'Blue Balls' DeMarco watched as two girls lathered each other in blue and yellow paint and slid sexily around. Blue Balls was still a virgin, hence the nom de plume, but he was working his way up to it. One day he hoped to ask a girl out, face to face, maybe take her to dinner, see what happens.

Next to Blue Balls, Paulie 'The Blind Man' Carvalho sucked spaghetti into his mouth from a large plate. At least he thought it was spaghetti. That was the thing about blind people; you could feed them worms in tomato sauce and they simply wouldn't know the difference. Paparella mostly felt sorry for the guy. What was the point in visiting a strip club if you couldn't see the goods on display? You might as well stay at home, put some jazz on, and whack yourself off whilst simultaneously crying into your braille pornography. *Two dots and a dash for a tit, two dashes and a dot for a growler.*

Playing the pinball machine at the side of the stage was Luca 'Hebeshebe' Brazzia. Paparella still wasn't sure about Luca. Was it a man, was it a woman? Was it both? Were there working parts in that downstairs region, and if so could one reach the other? Luca was a fine hitman/hitwoman, and that was all that mattered to Paparella. Who cared what it was, so long as it took out the marks it was assigned to and sank the evidence with concrete-slippers in the Thames?

"Don Paparella," a voice said, its speaker so close to his ear that he felt the brush of stubble upon his lobe. He turned to find, standing there with a concerned expression, a man he had not expected to see in his club tonight, or ever, for that matter.

"Detective Inspector Tyler," Paparella said, easing himself up from his seat and turning to face the man. "Well, this *is* a surprise. I didn't think you detective types were into this kind of thing? Spaghetti and sex shows is a strange combination, I know, but it works, don't you think?"

The DI glanced over his shoulder at the men seated at the oval table. He looked nervous, Don Paparella thought. And as well he should, coming in her unannounced. "I need to talk to you about Ted Barker."

Don Paparella scratched his head. "Who?"

"You know damn well who, Paparella," DI Tyler said. "The man whose face you exploded earlier today."

"Doesn't ring a bell," Paparella said. *God I'm good*, he thought. *Like, good enough to be a lawyer. Good enough to star in Home and Away. Good enough to change my name to Robert DeNiro and start making subpar romantic comedies alongside Jennifer Aniston or Kate Beckinsale.*

The detective-inspector sighed. "You're a good actor, Paparella," he said. "Like, good enough to star in *Neighbours*, or even *TOWIE*, but I see straight through you, and I can only cover up so much of your mess. This isn't Boston, Paparella. This isn't the Wild West, and it sure as hell ain't Weston-Super-Mare. You kill someone in Chiswick, people are going to notice, and I can't keep making it all go away, brushing it under the carpet like a dried bogey or a piece of old sandwich."

"That's incredibly graphic," said Paparella. And then his demeanour changed from one of comfortable serenity to almost unmitigated rage. His face turned purple—or maybe that was the disco lights dancing across his features—and his bottom lip shot out. "How fucking dare you come into my place of business and tell me what I can and can't do," he said. All eyes in the place turned to him and the detective-inspector, including Paulie 'The Blind Man' Carvalho's, and his didn't even work properly. "And I don't appreciate being accused of whacking someone off, either," he went on. "Those are very serious allegations, Tyler, allegations which I don't think you have any evidence to substantiate. Am I correct?"

DI Tyler was frozen with fear, suddenly very aware of where he was and who he was messing with. "I, erm, I don't know what, erm, they've found at the scene, erm—" He was like a child, berated for one too many skid-marks in his boxers.

Thumbs and Baby-Teeth had left their game of *Guess Who?* and were now standing directly behind Tyler. "This prick causing you trouble, boss?" Thumbs said.

DI Tyler turned around, about to explain why he wasn't a prick and that, even if he were, he wouldn't dare keep it up in front of Don Paparella, because he cherished his kneecaps. They went very well with his shins and calves, and it would be a shame to see what they would look like after a hammer attack.

"Everything's under control," Paparella said. Tyler sighed, turned back to face the capo. "DI Tyler and I were just discussing how he would receive a rather generous bonus if he made the taxidermist problem go away."

Tyler's face lit up—or maybe that was the disco-lights dancing across his features (a recycled joke is oftentimes better than none at all)—and he seemed to relax a little. "A bonus?" he said. "For making the taxidermist problem go away?"

"Who am I? Huh? Woody Woodpecker?" Don Paparella asked the two hulking brutes to the rear of Tyler. "Did I stutter?" Thumbs and Baby-Teeth shook their heads. To Tyler, Paparella said, "If your boys find any evidence that we were anywhere near that two-bit mausoleum, I want you to make sure it disappears, capiche?"

DI Tyler nodded. He was already spending the bonus in his head: his wife was always prattling on about how she hadn't been abroad in almost ten years; he would send her—as far away as possible—to the destination of her choice. He had always wanted to eat at the new fancy restaurant in town, Thai Tanic (goes down a treat!), and he could do that while his wife was away. And there were two old prossers he'd fancied a go at; he'd seen them sitting at the bar in The Swan with Two Tits. After his visit to Thai Tanic, he could pop in there, donk them both over the head with his truncheon, and drag them back to his wifeless house for a round of How's Your Father and a packet of prawn cocktail crisps, his favourite post-coital snack for some reason or other.

"I said 'capiche'?" Paparella repeated.

"Capiche," Tyler said. "Anything you say. Just… just don't go whacking any more people off, okay? I can only do so much on my side." *If the bonus is big enough,* he thought, *I might even treat myself to a new barbecue, one of the ones with multiple hobs and one of those crazy little rotisserie thingamajigs.* "Is there any chance I can get some of that bonus up front?" He knew he was pushing his luck, but the thought of getting rid of his wife for a few weeks while he played hide the sausage with a pair of right dirty MILFs was too much.

Paparella frowned. "Are you telling me your boys found some evidence?"

Tyler nodded. "Evidence, you say? Oh, yes, they found a lot of evidence. So much evidence you wouldn't believe. They've got evidence coming out their ears."

"Like what?" Paparella said, seemingly unconvinced. His face had returned to its normal hue—or maybe it was the disco-lights NOT dancing across his face—and he'd tucked his bottom lip back in.

"Liiiiike…" Tyler knew he was clutching at straws, but the bonus was slipping away from him, and the only way he was going to get it back was by lying like a politician on April 1st. "Fingerprints!" he said. "You left so many fingerprints at the scene, so, so many."

"Not me," Thumbs said.

"Yours were the *worst!*" Tyler said, turning to face the big fella. "Your thumbprints are like maps of the underground. The boys in the lab won't know whether to process them or play hopscotch on them."

"Thumbs doesn't have a police record, do you, Thumbs?" Paparella said.

"Apart from *Message in a Bottle*," Thumbs said, shaking his head, "they were shit."

"But you do!" Tyler said to Paparella. "You have a record longer than this chapter, don't you?"

The capo smiled and shrugged: *Eh, whadacanIsay! Iamabidofascoundrel!*

"I can make those prints disappear from forensics,"

Tyler said. "I've got access to them, and I'm the only person standing between you and a possible twenty-stretch, or worse—community service."

"Please make those prints disappear," Paparella said, dropping the fake Italian for a moment. His true accent made Ray Winstone sound like the Earl of Sandwich. He reached into his trouser pocket and came out with a roll of notes big enough to choke a llama. Tyler was about to get very excited when he saw the roll was comprised of only fives. There was probably two-hundred quid there, if you were lucky, and the sonofabitch was pulling notes from the roll one at a time. He'd be lucky if this rather generous bonus was anything over thirty-five nicker. That wasn't even enough for the whores, let alone a bowl of Pad Thai.

"Here you go," Paparella said, handing over four of the notes, or twenty pound to those keeping count. "Don't go spending it all at once."

While it wasn't even enough for *one* of the whores followed by a bowl of Tom Yum Goong, it was money for nothing, since there wasn't any evidence at the lab to hide.

"If you want the rest of your bonus," Paparella said, "it's in the till at that Cat Rescue Charity Shop in town. If you swing by in the morning, I'm sure the old trout running the place will oblige you. Tell her Don Paparella sent you to collect."

A charity shop? Tyler thought. *Fantastic. That'll be three-pound-fifty, bringing my grand total to twenty-three-pound-fifty, for those keeping still keeping count.*

"Do you want us to pick him, carry him to the entrance, and throw him out so that he lands in a puddle?" Baby-Teeth said.

"I'm sure the detective can find the exit of his own volition," Paparella said. "And besides, it's not raining."

DI Tyler left GANGSTER'S PARADISE (girls required! Cash in hand. Pole experience preferred but not essential) less than a minute later, cursing under his breath and checking over both shoulders to make sure he wasn't being followed.

13

The shop was dark, its goods limned by the moonlight, and the dead old lady—now living in the store cupboard at the back of the room—had finally stopped farting. Out on the street beyond the large windows, drunken men walked back and forth between pubs and clubs like zombies, groaning incomprehensibly and drooling into their salt-and-pepper beards. They had wives at home, of course, waiting, but would rather mill about in the dark than return to them, for the barrel-load of fucks they would receive due to their inebriation seemed a fate worse than dead.

While the pissed-up zombies traipsed along the cobbles out front, the dead animals were finally getting some much-needed rest. Jemima-Jessica were snoring over in one corner. Jemima's snore was a dainty little thing, like tinny windchimes during a summer breeze, while Jessica sounded like Bobcat Goldthwait having several orgasms all at the same time. Up in the far corner, Hooter had found a suitable branch upon which to stand, though it wasn't a branch at all, but a pneumatic door bracket, and if someone came through that door in that moment, the owl's legs would be ripped off at the ankles, but since the only person in the adjacent room was the dead old lady, the chances of that happening were slim to none.

Gerry had opted to sleep behind the counter unit, since he was technically a baby—had been for decades now—and was terrified of wetting himself publically, despite not passing urine since the day he died due to the fact he no longer had a bladder or took on water. To wet the bed in his current state would be a wonder, to shit it would be a bona fide miracle. But were they not walking-talking taxidermy? Proof that miracles do indeed happen? By contrast, an accidental defecation could be considered uninteresting.

Vladimir, who had been indefatigably unicycling for most of the day, had finally succumbed to sleep. He dreamt of Vodka and bears, bears drinking vodka, bears dreaming of vodka, and while the dreams were undeniably soviet—President Putin punching a bear in the ball-sack whilst singing Tatu's *All The Things She Said*' coming a close second—if you were to ask the rat in the morning he would tell you he'd much rather have dreamt of two lady-rats having it off.

Fairfax was the only dead animal not sleeping, for he was still coming to terms with his astounding reanimation and didn't want to jinx it by nodding off only to wake, half-eaten by dogs, in a farmer's field.

But this all felt so real. It couldn't be a dream, could it? He was really here, wasn't he?

And what a crazy menagerie he had become part of. A racist owl, a Russian rat, a two-headed duck, and a baby giraffe; his mother would be turning in her grave about now, if she'd *had* one and not been buried bit by bit by an overly-excited Chihuahua.

And if this *was* real, were they actually going to face up to gangsters tomorrow? Gangsters with guns and quasi-Italian accents? Fairfax hadn't been dead long, but even he knew there were risks involved.

"Can't sleep, huh?"

Fairfax looked up, heart in his throat, and saw the owl staring down at him, the faint hint of a smile tugging at the corner of its mouth. "It's rather strange," Fairfax whispered so as not to wake the others, "but one is still pumped up following the day's events." *Not to mention the fact that there's a rigid geriatric in the next room*, he thought but didn't add.

The owl sighed. "You know, I didn't mean what I said earlier… about you being—"

"A gingerbollocks?" Fairfax said. "No, you were well within your rights. One does have bollocks, and they are incredibly ginger—"

"About not being one of us," Hooter finished.

"You're here, you saw what those Ities did to our creator, you're as much a part of us as I am."

Fairfax nodded. "Well, one is moved by your admission," he said, adjusting his monocle and trying not to look like a prat at the same time. "But one is also confused as to what is going to happen tomorrow when those Mafiosos arrive here. Are we going to fight them? If so, shouldn't we be arming ourselves. Shouldn't there be a montage, with 1980's beats, while we set traps about the place and while one smears camouflage paint upon one's ginger phizzog?"

"That's not a bad idea," Hooter said. "Do you think we should wake the others and do that?"

"Let them sleep awhile," Fairfax said. "80's montages usually only take three minutes or so. We'll have plenty of time for one in the morning, should we rise early."

Hooter nodded his head, which was unusual since they usually just bob up and down or swivel side to side. But this was a proper nod; a human nod.

"I never asked," said Fairfax, "and you don't have to go into it if it's too painful, but how did you end up stuffed?" He wasn't sure if dragging up such an awful event was the way forward in this particular conversation, but it was better than an awkward silence.

"Flew into a window," Hooter said, matter-of-factly. "Went straight into it at full-pelt. Left a perfect outline of myself on the double-glazing." He paused, perhaps thinking back to that tragic day, the day of his own demise, and sighed. "You know what the worst part about it was? As I lay dying, twitching like a shitting dog and choking on my own beak, the owners of the house—Pakistani, they were—came out to see what all the commotion was, and when they saw me, on my death-bed, they didn't discuss which vet they were going to call or their own knowledge of owl CPR. They laughed. They made a big joke about the stupid owl slamming into their window, and, oh, look at this! A perfect outline of the dying owl on the glass! How hilarious!"

Fairfax clicked his tongue. "That's awful," he said. "One can only imagine how that felt."

"Humans are wankers, mate, and these ones were the worst."

"Do you think that's where your casual racism comes from?" It was, Fairfax thought, a fair question.

Hooter shrugged. "Nah, I was pretty racist before that happened. I was leader of my local National Front chapter. We used to gather on Thursdays and Sundays to slag off Bill Cosby and black cats."

"The Bill Cosby thing is probably understandable," said Fairfax, "but one has fornicated with plenty of black cats, and they are quite nice."

There was an uncomfortable silence in which Fairfax pondered whether he'd used his best and only question too soon and Hooter tried to shake the image from his mind of Fairfax bumming a black tom. After several minutes—the annoying second-hand carriage-clock on the shelf ticked them off quite loudly—Fairfax faked a yawn.

The owl followed suit. "Night, Fairfax," he said.

"Night, Hooter," Fairfax said.

Hooter's head spun away so that it faced the door. Fairfax tried to do the same and, following an audible crack and a whimper, decided to sleep the way he always had.

*

"We shouldn't be here," Murtow said as Ricks worked away at the lock with an old paperclip and a piece of chewing-gum. He only succeeded in making a helluva mess. As Ricks untangled the gum from his fingers, Murtow said, "Do you even know what you're doing?"

Popping the gum back into his mouth, Ricks said, "Saw MacGyver do it once. Thought it was worth a shot."

I'm too old for this shit, Murtow thought but didn't say. He didn't want it to become a catchphrase. Bruce Wallis, one of the lads over on Vice, had once used the phrase *Yippee-Ki-Yay, motherfudger!* during an arrest, and now the rest of his squad expected it all the time. They had even printed up tee-shirts and ceramic mugs with the slogan on. It was all very embarrassing, especially for Bruce Wallis, who had never fudged a mother before in his life.

The street was dark, save for a single light at one end, beneath which three married men had gathered to while away the hours so that they didn't have to return to their wives, who by now would be armed with rolling-pins, spatulas, and divorce papers. Murtow hated being out after dark. The city was a violent place at night. Just yesterday, an old lady was mugged outside the train station; the mug had the words *Yippee-Ki-Yay, motherfudger!* printed on one side and a picture of Bruce Wallis on the other.

"What's that?" Murtow said as Ricks pulled something from his jacket. "Is that a glass-cutter? Where the hell did you get a glass-cutter from?"

Ricks suctioned the glass-cutter to the shop's front window and began to draw a large circle with the blade. "Same place I get everything from," he said. "Amazon. Free postage, too, because it was more than ten quid." The blade squealed as it ripped through the glass. Murtow's false teeth vibrated in his face.

"Aren't they going to know we were here?" Murtow asked. "If we leave a bloody big circular hole in the front of the shop?"

Ricks stopped cutting for a moment. Clearly, he hadn't thought that far ahead. But that was the thing about Ricks. He was a maverick, a rebel, and some might say an absolute idiot. "We'll pop the glass back in when we're done," he said, resuming cutting. "No one will know the difference." The circle fell inwards, smashing into millions of tiny shards on the floor of BARKER'S STUFFED EMPORIUM (Dry-cleaning service available!).

"I'm too old for this shit," Murtow grumbled.

"You want to be careful," Ricks said. "That's starting

to sound like a catchphrase, and you know what happened to Arnie Schwarzenfinger over in accounting. He only said 'Get to the copier' twice, and now it's his official entrance music."

In through the window they climbed. "Do you think we should take out shoes and socks off?" Ricks said. "So we don't get any glass in our soles?"

"Go ahead," Murtow said. "I'm going to keep mine on, if you don't mind, so I don't get any glass in my bare feet."

"Good thinking," Ricks said, pulling his socks back on. "Okay, Murtow, we're looking for clues, anything that will lead to the whereabouts of Don Paparella and his gang of badfellas."

"You had to go there, didn't you?" Murtow said. "This story has been going on for a while now. I'm pretty sure that somewhere, at some point, someone has already used that gag."

"Bloody good gag," Ricks said.

"It's not even a gag," Murtow said, helping Ricks to climb back into his shoes. "It's barely even a pun." Once Ricks was dressed properly once again, they set about searching for clues, which was more difficult than it sounded since, although he had managed to remember to bring a glass-cutter along, Ricks had left his torch in his stockings drawer at home.

"What are we looking for again?" Murtow asked, picking up a blood-covered rug and lowering back down again once he was satisfied no one was hiding underneath it. "Those guys at Forensics are pretty good at their job, you know. If there was anything here to find, they would have—"

"That's where you're making a mistake," Ricks said, squinting through the dark. "You see, you're assuming that the guys in Forensics are good, honest, hard-working cops like us, but this goes deep, Murtow. Much deeper than you think. It's got police corruption written all over it—"

"You found something with police corruption written all over it?" Murtow said. He sounded quite distant. "Burn it! Burn it before you read it! No good can come from—"

"I haven't *found* a thing," Ricks said. "You're going to give yourself a coronary, keep going on like that. What I was saying was that I wouldn't be surprised if this goes all the way to the top. I'm talking the chief-superintendent, and I don't trust DI Tyler as far as I can throw him."

"You think Paparella's got help from the force?" Murtow said, sounding somewhat dubious.

"Oh, come on!" Ricks said. "Paparella's waltzed into Chiswick with a few good men and managed to extort fifty percent of the place, including the fines department at the station. Tyler's not doing a damn thing about it, and just today he told us to keep out of it. You know why he said that?"

Murtow grunted. "Because we usually cause several thousand pounds' worth of damage and end up being punched in the face or held hostage. Excessive force complaints are up ten-fold since we started working together. We're not exactly pillars of the community. Maybe that's why Tyler told us to keep our beaks out."

"Maybe," Ricks said, riffling through a series of desk drawers, which seemed to contain glinting implements of varying shape and size. It looked to Ricks like the contents of Jeffrey Dahmer's lunchbox. There was nothing in there of any use. "Or maybe he doesn't want us sullying his reputation. Maybe he's scared what we'll discover."

"If you're right, we could be OWWWW!" Murtow howled.

"Murtow?" Ricks said, suddenly concerned. His partner was on the verge of death, and so Ricks always took an OWWWW! To mean I'M DYING! I'M ACTUALLY DYING!

Murtow was hopping around the room, cursing under his breath and hissing through his teeth. Ricks could just about make out his partner's shape as he first went one way, and then the other. Something clattered to the ground as Murtow ploughed into the wall. And then there was a deep and long grunt.

"Stumped your toe?" Ricks asked.

"I have, Ricks," Murtow said. "However, that noise wasn't me."

"What do you mean it wasn't you?"

"I mean," spat Murtow, "that while I am in absolute agony, that long groan wasn't me. There is someone else in the room with us."

"Ten points to the good cop!" a voice groaned. "I can see why you're a police officer."

"Who's there!" Murtow said, spinning in the semi-darkness trying to locate the source of the voice. "I'm too old for this shit!"

"You knocked me of the fucking wall!" said the voice. "I think my horn's crooked."

Ricks moved through the dark like lightning, chopping at thin air with his hand. "I know kung-fu!" he cried. "You'd better lie down on the floor and stay there, otherwise I won't be held responsible for any damage to your personage."

"I *am* lying on the floor!" bellowed the voice. It was close; somewhere down by Ricks's feet, in fact. "Your stupid partner backed into me. Do you have any idea how embarrassing this is? I've never been on a floor before. It's not a nice place for a head to be."

Ricks began kicking manically, hoping to catch the voice in the face. "Murtow! Do you see it?"

"I can't see a damn thing!" Murtow said, followed by, "I think my toenails hanging off."

Ricks dropped to his knees and began to crawl around, like a drunken man looking for his car-keys, even though the landlord had confiscated them just a moment ago. "I've got a particular set of skills!" Ricks warned. "I will find you, and I will arrest you!"

"That's all well and good," said the voice, "but how's that going to straighten my horn? Decades I've managed without so much as a scratch. You pair come in here, and two minutes later I look like something from a Tim Burton movie. No wonder your superior told you not to get involved with this case. Leave now, before you have the whole place up in flames."

Somewhere to the right, Ricks thought. Very close… so very close. He crawled on hands and knees searching for the voice, rubbing his hand over the rug, occasionally touching something which probably should have been cleaned up by the Forensics Department—a bit of grey matter, perhaps, or a sliver of scalp.

"Murtow, do you have my lighter? The one with the red-headed woman on it. The one I lent you yesterday to light those stupid incense sticks, the ones you are convinced smell like fresh rain when actually they have more than an air of wet dog's scrotum about them?"

"Take your time," said the deep voice. "We've got all night, and it'll be well worth the wait to see the look on your faces."

"Here!" Murtow shuffled through the darkness, limping, wondering whether he should take himself off to A&E or tough it out.

A second later and Ricks had the lighter in his hand and was thumbing at the flint wheel. *Fffft. Fffffft. Fffffft-whoosh!*

Ricks was face to face with the bodiless buffalo head, which appeared to have come loose from its wooden mount. "Boo!" said the head, which wasn't the most original thing it could have said in that moment, but it had the desired effect.

Ricks moaned, unable to find any words. His terrified moan stretched on and on, and it wasn't until Murtow was standing next to him, patting him comfortingly on the shoulder, that he fell silent.

"What is it?" Murtow said. "Did you set fire to your mullet?"

"The… the fucking buffalo!" Ricks gasped through staccato breaths. "It… it's alive!"

Murtow stared down at the head, frowning, wondering whether Ricks had forgotten to take his medication that morning, despite Doctor Agrawal's warning that just one missed tablet could result in hallucinations, sore tummy, constipation, diarrhoea, headaches, nausea, weight gain, weight loss, mass-murder, dry mouth, and gout. "That is the deadest water buffalo I think I've ever seen, Ricks." Murtow didn't need this tonight, his partner going off the deep end. He needed Ricks focussed, not babbling on about some—

"You must be the sensible one," said the buffalo to Murtow. "What's your catchphrase? I bet you've got a really good one."

Murtow went down clutching his chest, unconscious and already dreaming of his wife's home-baked bread.

*

Voices. Two voices, one much deeper than the other. Murtow slowly opened his eyes and smacked his lips together, for his mouth was dryer than a dead dingo's dong. Even though his eyes were now open, he still couldn't see a thing. The room he was in was dark, filled with shadows and not much else. The voices were conversing, laughing, back and forth, jovial. Murtow was just glad he hadn't shit himself.

"Hey, Ricks," he grunted, his voice hoarse and his throat sore, as if he had swallowed—been force-fed—razorblades as he snoozed. "Ricks."

The voices stopped talking, and then the deeper of the two said, "Oh, look who's back in the room."

Murtow didn't recognise the voice, but something about it reminded him of *Seven Brides for Seven Brothers.* "Howard Keel?" Murtow said. "Is that you?"

Ffffft… Ffffft… Fffft-whoosh…

One corner of the room lit up and, sitting there around an invisible campfire, were Ricks and the bodiless water buffalo. Ricks looked happy; the buffalo looked unsurprisingly odd and out of place. It all came flooding back to Murtow. The water-buffalo without a body could speak! It could speak, and now it was sitting across the room, chatting nonchalantly to his partner as if it were the most normal thing in the world, and Ricks was chatting back to it when he should have probably been putting his foot through it as hard as he possibly could.

"Fngh," Murtow said, and then he went back to sleep.

*

When he opened his eyes this time, the room was a little lighter, and so was the object in Ricks's hand. "Morning, Murtow," Ricks said, far too cheerfully for Murtow's liking. Panic washed over him as he fought to make sense of what was going on. Where was Tash? Why hadn't he woken up next to his beautiful wife, with the children bouncing on the bed and cracking rude jokes about him being a dinosaur? Why was Ricks here, and what was that strange burning smell?

"Ow!" Murtow said, patting out the flames which engulfed his eyebrows. He knocked the lighter from his partner's hand and sat upright, straining to see through blurry, sleep-filled eyes. Focusing on the mullet, he said, "Where are we? What the hell is going on, Ricks?"

"You don't remember?" Ricks said, almost mockingly. "Last night we became a trio. An incongruous triangle of mayhem, Murtow. Don't you see, this is the best chance we've got of bringing down Paparella and his bozos. He's going to help us, Murtow. Bill's going to join us on our quest."

Murtow frowned, knitting his smoking eyebrows together. "Bill?" he said. "Who the hell is Bill?"

Ricks turned around, and there, strapped to his back was the head of a water-buffalo. "Sorry about last night," the head said. "You're pretty squeamish for a 1980's law-enforcement stereotype."

Murtow was halfway to the ground when Ricks grabbed him and held him steady. "We don't have time for any more sleeping," he said. "Murtow, there are more out there. More like Bill. And they're going after Paparella."

"We used to be inseparable," Bill's voice said from behind Ricks, "but apparently, they could handle this one without me, which is fine, since I've got lots of better things to be getting on with."

"It's… it's a…" Murtow took a deep breath to compose himself. When he next spoke, his voice was steady. "Ricks, you have a talking head strapped to your back. The head of a water-buffalo which should, beyond any shadow of a doubt, *not* be talking." Ricks nodded manically, his smile wide and filled with childlike wonder, which was not the best trait for a forty-year-old policeman to have. "And the head, Ricks, has told you that there are more like it out there? Hunting down Don Paparella, the most ruthless crime boss London has seen since Piers Morgan pissed off to America? Is that what you're telling me, Ricks, just so I have it straight in my head."

Ricks nodded. "Bill's a good head," he said. "I think he'll be useful to us, and he really wants to be reunited with his friends. Apparently, we just missed them yesterday. They were in a bit of a rush, which is why Bill here was left behind."

Murtow wasn't certain, but he thought he heard a quiet sniffle at the rear of Ricks.

"And look on the bright side," Ricks said, patting his partner hard on the shoulder. "You're not going crazy. The water-buffalo did mouth 'Bruce Willis' yesterday.

You were absolutely right about that."

"Good to know," Murtow said, his left eye twitching recurrently. "Ricks, can I have a word with you in private?"

"I've just strapped him on," Ricks said. And then, when he saw the expression on Murtow's face, to the water-buffalo he said, "Bill, just cover your ears for a minute, will you? We're going to have a private chat. You do have ears, don't you? I'm not familiar with your anatomy."

The deep voice from Ricks's rear said, "Of course I have ears. I'm a bovid, not a burns victim."

"Hah!" Ricks said. "Very funny. And also more than a little controversial. I like that about you, Bill."

"You're going to love Hooter then," said Bill. "Okay, my ears are covered. Go ahead and talk about me. See if I care."

Murtow checked to make sure the water-buffalo was telling the truth before continuing. "Are you out of your damn mind, Ricks!" he half-whispered, half-shouted. "You're seriously suggesting we take that… that *thing* with us? On this case?"

"We need an annoying sidekick," Ricks said. "That's how this works. The straight man, the slightly unhinged action hero, and the irritating tag-along. We've landed on our feet with this one—"

"But the buffalo hasn't," Murtow said, "because it doesn't damn well have any feet, does it? Do you see how wrong that is, Ricks? Do you see why I'm a little cranky?"

Ricks considered what his partner was saying, nodding along, more for dramatic effect than anything else. "Bill saw his creator gunned down in cold blood," he finally said. "He saw Paparella pull the trigger, and knows what the lunatic looks like. He also told me that we're looking for a man with a mouth full of baby teeth and a man with nothing but thumbs for hands. That's the kind of information money can't buy, even in this city."

Murtow shuddered. *That's the kind of information I don't need to hear right now*, he thought. A man with just thumbs for hands? Whatever next? A gangster with Irritable Bowel Syndrome?

"We can nail this sonofabitch," Ricks said, whispering conspiratorially. "We'll get medals of valour for this, Murtow. We'll make the papers. We'll be captains by the end of the week!"

"We'll be lucky if we get a free Cornish pasty and a three-shot cappuccino," Murtow said, shaking his head. Nothing was getting through to Ricks; it seemed his partner had already made up his mind. But that was the thing about Ricks. He was a pummel someone half to death with his truncheon first, ask questions later kind of guy. Once he got something into his head, that was it. You might as well play along, and hope to God you didn't die in the process. "Okay," Murtow ceded. "So what's the plan, huh? What magnificent little strategy did you and the bodiless water-buffalo come up with while I was unconscious?"

The smile dropped from Ricks's face. "Hm, yeah, we probably had time to figure something out last night, didn't we? But Bill's an amazing chess player, except of course he can't move the pieces by himself, which is a little bit annoying as it seemed as if I was doing the lion's share of the work, but we had fun nonetheless, and we kind of lost track of time." He shrugged. "I guess what I'm saying is that we don't have a plan, per se, just an intense urge to get out there and find those murderous pricks before they kill again."

Murtow was lost for words, and when he was lost for words, six words automatically trickled from his lips to fill the silence. "I'm too old for this shit."

14

Martin Chuzzlechops wandered along the market, whistling, a spring in his step despite the ferocious hangover he had wakened to that very morning. It was a beautiful day, and his new haircut felt good on top of his head. People were stopping to stare, children were pointing and laughing. It felt good to be bringing so much joy to the people of Chiswick.

"What's your most expensive posey?" Martin said, stopping in front of a flower stall, its owner looking a little like a dead daffodil herself.

"What's that thing on top of your head?" the proprietor of the stall asked without humour.

Martin reached up and patted at the mass of wonder sitting atop his pate. "Ah, this is the haircut of all haircuts!" he said. "And so very nice of you to notice."

"Notice?" the woman said. "How could I bleedin' *not* notice? It looks like two skunks rutting. Is that the thing these days? All the rage, is it? Two skunks rutting?"

Martin shrugged, unsure whether to be offended or not. It was a beautiful day, and therefore nothing was going to bring him down. "About that posey…"

The woman bent down, disappearing behind a row of Kiss Me Over the Garden Gates, and when she returned clutching a fistful of purple flowers, she was grinning. "For a lady-friend, are they? Or do you just want something to overpower the smell of your haircut?"

"They're for my girlfriend," Martin said, smiling wistfully. "Her name is Ethel, and she… what was that about my hair?"

"Eighteen pound and ninety-nine pence," the woman said, handing Martin the posey, which didn't look as healthy as it had when it was further away. "If you want 'em wrapped, it'll be another three quid."

"No, I'm taking them straight to her," Martin said, the smile returning to his face. If he was lucky, Ethel would take him in the back room, pop her teeth out, and suck his—

"Ah! This fucking hag!" said a voice Martin recognised instantly as belonging to Don Paparella, the meanest fake-gangster in all of London. He turned to find the little capo, flanked by his much larger friends, standing there. The one with thumbs for hands was eating a Cornetto (other conical ice-creams are available, but they taste like shit!). The one with the teeth of a baby was chewing upon a strawberry swizzle. Red sugar fell from the sweet onto Don Paparella's shoulder, and the little gangster dusted it off, more than a little annoyed that he was being sprinkled. To the woman, who was now doing everything in her power not to make eye contact with Paparella, he said, "Half your takings, love, and a bunch of your finest red roses."

The woman set about serving the capo, and as she did, Martin Chuzzlechops put a twenty-pound note down on the counter and slowly edged away from the stall, not wanting to become part of the situation, for he was a big fan of kneecaps, especially the ones on his own body. Without them, he would simply buckle under the weight of his own torso, and that was not a good look for him.

Onwards he went, whistling tunelessly now, the hair on his head blowing gently in the breeze and looking more like a pair of fornicating skunks than ever before.

*

Reginald Cline, that poor, poor hobo, climbed from his box around nine. The day would be a better one, he surmised, with very little in the way of hallucinations. There would be no foxes today, no talking owls, and certainly no baby giraffes, two-headed ducks, or unicycling rats. It had all been a figment of his imagination, the result of some bad booze or a not-quite-right sandwich—affluent people got their kicks in strange ways, and serving a vagrant an off egg-mayo roll, Reginald thought, was not beyond them, the sick, twisted bastards.

But today Reginald felt rejuvenated. He had slept well enough, waking only twice in the night to shake the piss from his box. The weather was good, the smell of freshly-cooked bacon wafted through the streets from the myriad greasy spoons peppering the borough. Reginald didn't know which café to head for, Deja Brew (You'll keep coming back like it's the first time!) or Lard Have Mercy! (Heart-attacks are our thing!). Since the two establishments were next to one another, it didn't really matter. Reginald began walking in their general direction, grunting as passers-by on the off-chance at least one of them had a bit of change to spare.

Arriving at the cafés, Reginald positioned himself on the ground between the two. Taking out his cardboard sign, upon which were scrawled the words "Breakfast would be nice…", he placed it down by his feet next to his collection cup, upon which was printed the slogan *"Yippee Ki-Yay, motherfudger!"* for some reason or other. On the other side was a picture of a man who looked a little like Bruce Willis, but wasn't quite him. Reginald had found the cup in the bin. *The things people throw away*, he thought.

"Spare some change for a breakfast?" he asked a passing woman. The woman ignored him, made her way into Deja Brew to feed her own fat face, and to hell with the poor, poor starving man propped up against the café's exterior.

At least I'm not mad, Reginald reminded himself, and that was true, and he was grateful for it. Yesterday he was destined for the nut-house, but, he'd assured himself at the time, there had to be a reasonable explanation for what he had just witnessed. Animals don't talk, foxes don't dress like they're on the way to an Edwardian orgy, and rats don't ride unicycles. No, what he had witnessed were regular animals—if they had even been there at all—and his mind had played a trick upon him, which it was wont to do on occasion. Lack of proper food, an overdose of cheap battery-acid cider, and a cigarette made from fifteen other cigarette butts did strange things to a man's psyche.

Like conjuring up the cast of Farthing Wood, for starters.

A shadow suddenly fell upon Reginald. Without looking up, he said, "Spare some change?" He tapped the *Yippee-Ki-Yay, motherfudger!* cup with his holey shoe.

"You do realise that begging is illegal," said a voice. "Punishable by up to a year in jail, or a fifty pound fine, whichever you prefer."

Reginald looked nervously up to find two men standing before him. One of them, the white one, seemed to be wearing some sort of poncho across his shoulders. The black one, much older by the looks of him, seemed to be a little embarrassed by his friend's behaviour, and was muttering under his breath something about being far too advanced of years for this nonsense.

"Just trying to scrape together enough for breakfast," Reginald said, appealing to the mulleted one. "Are you policemen?"

"We are," said the white one. "But we're undercover at the moment." He winked at Reginald, and Reginald winked back, for he didn't know what else to do. "Don't go telling anyone you saw us."

"I won't," said Reginald. "Providing you put three-pound-ninety-five in my cup, and another pound for a pot of tea." He held the cup out toward the undercover cops and gave it a gentle shake. Its contents—a euro, a dollar, five francs, and a button from an old coat— rattled noisily around.

"Hey, isn't that…" The black cop pointed at the mug.

The white cop leaned in and examined the face on the side of the mug. "Yep. Getting around a bit, isn't he? Maybe you should have a catchphrase after all, Murtow."

"*Murtow*, is it?" Reginald said, lowering the mug for a moment. "I thought you were undercover? Wouldn't it make sense to go by an alias? John Doe, perhaps, or Alan Smithee, the greatest director that ever did live?"

The black cop dead-armed his partner. "Couldn't keep your mouth shut, Ricks, could you? Now he knows my name. You've blown our cover and we've only been up ten minutes. We'll be strapped to a ceiling, feet in water, being electrocuted by an angry china-man by lunchtime at this rate."

"Not if you put three-pound-ninety-five in my mug," Reginald reminded them, "and another pound for a pot of tea."

The white cop began to fumble for the change in his pockets. Somewhere nearby, a third voice said, "Don't give the bugger any money," but Reginald couldn't locate the source of the voice and, besides, he was used to such negativity. *He'll only blow it all on drugs and drink*, people would say, to which he would reply, *You try sleeping in a bit of cardboard for ten years and see how sober you want to be.*

"Here you go," the mulleted cop said, dropping the coinage into Reginald's mug. "Get yourself an extra rasher of bacon, but you didn't see us, okay?"

Reginald nodded. "I didn't see you," he said, even though he very much had. "Ta very much."

The cops—who looked to be channelling some kind of terrible action movie from the 1980s, what with the stereotypical black/white sensible/nutty ensemble—continued on their merry way, and Reginald watched them go.

And as they went, the poncho strapped to the mulleted cop lifted ever-so-slightly, and Reginald recoiled in horror as a hairy face, its tongue bobbing out in a raspberry, stared back at him.

And that was, as they say, the straw which broke the camel's back. Reginald decided to check himself into

Broadmoor at the nearest available opportunity, before he did himself, or the general public, any real damage.

*

DI Tyler marched through the streets, a man on a mission, and that mission was to collect the rest of his bonus from the old lady, Ethel Gripe, at the Cat Rescue Charity Shop. He knew Ethel well, since she had been arrested on many occasions, mainly for protesting against animal-testing on felines, occasionally for stealing her next-door neighbour's Avon delivery, and once for punching a Down's Syndrome child in the face. The last offence, according to Ethel, had been self-defence, but Tyler suspected it was more to do with the fact that the kid was trying to steal a book on wildlife—*Great English Tits: An Illustrated Guide*—from the shop.

She was a feisty one, was Ethel Gripe, and Tyler knew he was in for a rough morning, for she wouldn't allow him to procure half the shop's takings without putting up at least a little fight.

Damn you, Paparella, he thought as he stepped over a homeless man who seemed to be drooling into a mug and babbling something about a man with horns and a hairy face.

*

Martin Chuzzlechops arrived at the charity-shop and, following a quick breath-test—yeah, it stunk like an anus—he gave the posey a cursory once-over and stepped inside.

The little bell hanging over the door tinkled as he

143

eased it shut behind him. "Ethel?" he called out when he saw she wasn't standing like a Victorian ghost in her usual place behind the counter. "Ethel? I've got a surprise for you, you sexy old so-and-so." He made his way into the shop proper, and that was when he started to smell something amiss. Even over the scent of the flowers he could taste it at the back of his throat; like old cake, it was, mixed with the ground-up remains of a thousand cockroaches. "Ethel, dear, have you had another accident?"

No answer.

A moment of sheer terror struck Martin. What if she was dead? His beloved Ethel, his sugarmomma (sugargranna?) lying dead somewhere in the vicinity? No, that couldn't be! *Ethel Gripe*, he assured himself, *is the healthiest woman I know, if you ignore the dodgy hips which click when we make love, the windy bottom which toots when we make love, the loose-fitting dentures, which fall out when we make love, and the strange amount of lubrication she generates when we make love. Ignore all of those things, and Ethel Gripe is as fit as a fiddle, and twice as bendy.*

"Ethel!" he called out once again. He made his way across the room, placed the posey down on the counter next to the till, and continued on toward the room at the back of the shop.

It was where they kept the stuff yet to be priced up. Ethel usually had someone in to do that for her—Mindy Mong loved that job, and had been doing it for as long as Ethel and Martin had been together—so it was strange to imagine Ethel back there, holding a pricing gun and going at the tattered books and knick-knacks like a woman possessed.

"Mindy?" Martin called. "Ethel?" The smell grew worse the nearer he got to the door. Whatever was making that stink was on the other side, hopefully not with its knickers around its ankles and an ashamed expression on its face. Not that Martin minded cleaning up after his other half; it was just something he shouldn't be doing at the ripe old age of forty-two.

"Okay, I'm coming in!" he said. "And Ethel, before I do, I want you to know that this isn't going to change anything between the two of us, okay? We've been through this before, and it's not a problem." Getting the filth from under his fingernails afterwards was something of a problem, but he didn't mention it.

He pushed the door-handle down and eased the door open slowly, so as not to startle Ethel, who may or may not have heard him, depending on whether she had her hearing-aids on.

It was like opening an oven door, only instead of heat rushing out, an almost hellish stench did instead. Martin was almost knocked from his feet as the reek hit him, went straight through him, did a three-point-turn and then came back at him again. By this point his eyes were watering so badly that he could barely see an inch in front of him, however he could just about make out the shape of a person sitting across the room, rocking back and forth on what appeared to be a creaky old rocking-chair.

"Gahethel!" he managed, swallowing bile back down and plugging his nostrils with his fingers. "Gethel, thish ith geh worsth one yeth." And it *was* the worst one yet; Martin just hoped it hadn't seeped into her tights like last time.

He entered slowly, rubbing at his watery eyes. Ethel didn't acknowledge him, which would have been nice, since he'd just spent twenty pound on a bunch of flowers which didn't stand a chance in the charity-shop's current climate. "Ethel?" he said, close enough now to see his sugargranna's face. Her mouth was wide open, her lips blue, her eyes bulging from their sockets like two snooker balls wedged into a pair of anuses. The first thing Martin thought was, *That must have been one hell of an accident.* The second thing he thought was, *Shit, she's dead! She's not breathing, she's dead!*

For a moment he was unable to speak. His mouth opened and shut, but nothing emerged, and he stood there looking down on the nonagenarian, angry with her for dying, especially after he'd just handed over his last twenty for flowers. Eventually, almost three whole minutes later—he knew it was three minutes because of the rather annoying carriage clock in the next room, loudly ticking off the seconds—he said, "Oh, Ethel! My darling! You would have loved my new haircut, and the flowers I bought for you! Oh, Ethel! I'm going to miss our sexy time! Our incredibly squelchy sexy time!" He knew he had to call someone. The police, perhaps, or should he go directly to the morgue? Throw the old lady over his shoulder and deliver her to McKenzie's Mortuary over on Bilbrook?

If he was going to do that, he might as well set fire to her himself, right here, right now. It's what she would have wanted, he surmised. She always said she wanted to be cremated; probably not petrol-bombed, the way Martin was thinking of doing it, but set on fire nonetheless.

"Oh, I don't know what to do, Ethel!" he said. This was all too much for him to take, and yet he should have expected it. Ethel Gripe had already defied science by making it this far (most people would be happy with sixty-five, in this day and age, but some people are just greedy). The last thirty years had been a bonus; the old bat better have made a will, he thought.

Martin reached into his pocket and pulled out his mobile phone. He was in the process of dialling the London Probate Department (where there's a will, there's a way!) when, all of a sudden, something barrelled into his legs. He toppled to the floor, rolled several times, and came to a stop lying on his back.

"Whathefuc—"

"Hit him again, Gerry!" a voice said.

"Are we sure he works for Paparella?" said another voice.

"Look at him!" said a third. "He's a gangster's lackey, if ever I saw one!"

Staring up at the ceiling, temporarily unable to move,

Martin Chuzzlechops said, "If you're going to hit me again, be careful of the hair. I just got it yesterday."

Then, a strange face appeared above him, looming over him like the world's ugliest dentist. It looked like a giraffe, but clearly he was mistaken. Giraffe's don't talk.

"Lights out," said the giraffe, and then it reared up, and cloven hooves came down hard on Martin's face.

The darkness was instant, but the voices lingered for a while, and he heard one of them declare, in broken English: "Look at way his ear hang off."

Then he was out cold, and not a moment too soon, as far as he was concerned.

*

"I don't think he's a gangster," Hooter said, gazing down on the man now strapped to the chair. The chair was far too small for him, its cartoon character design suggesting its intended age-range was three-to-seven. "Not with that haircut."

"It look like two skunk fucking," said Vladimir. "If there is more gangster-appropriate hairdo, I don't know what it is."

"The owl might very well be correct," Fairfax said, evaluating the man in the chair, circling him casually, and occasionally stopping to adjust his waistcoat. "One might even assume this poor fellow is the old lady's lover."

"Sick bastard!" Jemima said. "He's been shagging a dead lady?"

Fairfax clicked his tongue, for such a statement was

worthy of derision. "Of course, he was a lover to the old lady while she was still alive."

"That's even worse!" Jessica said, appalled. "We should murder him on general principal.

"I'm with two-headed duck on this one," Vladimir said. "This man is sick. We would be doing favour by putting out of misery."

"While you're probably correct that this man has issues," Fairfax said, "I don't think he's doing anything illegal, and I'm not terribly certain he had any association with Don Paparella and the Brentford mafia." He stood on two feet, scratched behind his ear, and said, "Yes, I'm almost positive this man is innocent, and should be released at the first available opportunity."

Hooter landed on the unconscious man's lap and, using his beak, tugged at the cloth restraints holding the man in place. "If this isn't the man we're waiting for," he said, "then we're wasting time. Those assholes could be on their way here right now, and we're in the stockroom trying to figure out what to do with a granny-fucker."

"Put him in the cupboard," Jemima said. "He'll sleep it off in there, and put the old lady in with him, just in case he wakes up and fancies cracking open a cold one—"

"You really are a most despicable creature," Jessica said, pecking at the identical head next to her own. "The man's just lost his girlfriend to a freak dead animal attack, and you're making jokes about necrophilia."

"Hey, if you can't joke about necrophilia, what *can* you joke about?" said Jemima.

"Gerry, take the pervert's legs," Fairfax said. "I've got his arms. On three… one… two…"

The sound of a tinkling bell stopped them in their tracks. Someone had just entered the shop.

The gangsters?

More perverts?

Fairfax and Gerry dropped the unconscious body and retook their hiding places along with the rest of the animals, just as a voice called out—

*

"Ethel Gripe! Ethel, you old sow, I'm here to collect on behalf of Don Paparella!" DI Tyler closed the door behind him and turned the sign to CLOSED. There was a strange smell in the air—like rotten pork mixed with the farts of a hundred men—and Tyler was grateful that he was suffering the tail-end of a cold, otherwise it might have been too much to bear. "Ethel, have you had an accident? Have you had an old-lady accident?" You didn't have to be a detective to know that women of Ethel Gripe's age were known for their sudden and violent evacuations. "Okay, Ethel, I'm just going to help myself to the till and then I'll be on my way, okay? No funny business. I don't want to have to arrest you." When no reply was forthcoming, DI Tyler decided it was good enough for him, and made his way across the room to the counter.

The till, much like its operator, was an old-fashioned thing. The buttons were large, no doubt intentionally so for those with failing vision, and there was a half-sucked mint humbug between the two and three, which Tyler wanted to avoid, if possible. "Okay, let's see how we do this," he muttered to himself, fingers hovering over the keypad. "No sale… no sale… no sale…"

He pushed the large blue button with TL/NS printed on it. NS, he guessed, meant No Sale. Made perfect sense. Unless it stood for Nova Scotia… National Service… Nasal Spray… Nephrotic Syndrome…

The till sprung open noisily, revealing a dusty cash drawer. Several of the compartments were empty, but one of them contained an unopened bag of coins, and while it was hardly a jackpot amount, a smile spread across DI Tyler's corrupt face. "Bingo," he said, which was precisely what he was going to spend the money on. He could turn this thirteen-pound-fifty into hundreds if he played his cards right. *Who's laughing now, Paparella?* Tyler thought as he took half the money from the bag and put the other half back.

"Ethel, I've taken half from the till!" he said, closing the cash register and making his way around the counter. "You did the right thing by not confronting me. I'll be sure to let Don Paparella know that you were compliant, and I won't mention your unfortunate little… smell problem." He snorted at that, for nothing tickled him more than the misfortunes of elderly folk. "I'll be on my way now," he said, moving toward the door and the clean air just beyond it. "Enjoy the rest of your day."

"You are not going anywhere, cocksucker!" a voice said.

DI Tyler turned around so fast that he almost severed his own penis on a clothing rail. There was, as far as he could see, no one else present. "Whosaidthat?" he gasped, for it certainly wasn't Ethel Gripe's voice. Maybe, he thought, it was Mindy Mong playing some kind of trick on him. She was like that, was Mindy. Mind of a ten-year-old, body of a fifty-year-old, breath of a dead person. "Is that you, Mindy?" Tyler asked, nervously scanning the shop for any signs of movement. "I'm on duty, and I will arrest you if I have to. Do you really want that, Mindy? To spend the day in a cold, dark cell?"

No reply.

"I didn't think so," Tyler said, relaxing once again. "Have a good day, and tell Ethel I said hel—"

"Tell her yourself, you corrupt piece of shit!" said the voice, and then something slammed into the back of DI Tyler, causing him to hurtle forwards, deep into the shop, toward the store cupboard at the back. He heard the flutter of wings, could feel the wind as they flapped above him, and then something had him by the collar and was pulling him toward the door.

He screamed.

The fox he passed on the way to the door screamed with him. *Eeeeeeeeeekkkkkk!*

He screamed so more as he was pushed forwards.

A small Russian voice said, "He make a lot of noise for policeman."

And then he was through the door, where he landed face-down on a grimy carpet. He quickly scrambled to his feet, and that was when he saw the bodies. Sitting in a rocking chair like Norman Bates' mother was Ethel Gripe. Judging by her hue, and the arm which stood upright in a perpetual rigor-mortis Nazi salute, she had been dead for a good few hours. Her eyes stared out at him, almost reproachfully, as if she blamed him for her death. At her feet, lying on his back, was Martin Chuzzlechops. Martin was breathing, but it was shallow, and his lip curled with every new breath he took. There was something dead on his head, too. It looked like a pair of fornicating skunks, but Tyler couldn't be sure.

"Not the prettiest couple in the world, are they?" said a voice down by Tyler's feet, and when he looked, saw the two-headed duck staring up at him, he did the first thing which came to mind. He kicked that fucking monster as hard as he could, watched as it flew through the air and collided with an art-deco wardrobe on the other side of the room.

"Now that's not very nice," said another voice. Tyler spun round, and when he saw the fox approaching—on two feet, no less, like a walking, talking human being, only ginger and wearing a waistcoat and a monocle— he knew he was in some nightmare parallel universe, which was really strange as he couldn't recall stepping through any wormholes or suchlike. "One suggests an apology to the two-headed duck would go a very long way indeed," said the fox.

"Gnghflenstein," Tyler muttered, which wasn't a real word but would have garnered a fantastic score in Scrabble.

"Heads up!" said a voice. DI Tyler turned just in time to see a barn owl swooping toward him, a weathered baseball bat clenched in its talons.

And then there came the inevitable metallic *donk!* and Tyler dropped like a sack of potatoes. He had never been knocked unconscious before in his life, and it wasn't as bad as he had been led to believe. Once the darkness came, it was pretty much plain-sailing, and though it could never be described as a pleasant sensation, he decided he would rather be temporarily comatose than inhabiting a nightmare world in which foxes wore pocket-watches and owls hit harder than Joe DiMaggio.

15

Ricks and Murtow arrived at THE PUSSY PALACE (you won't find any cats here!) at just after lunchtime. Lunch had consisted of hot-dogs from a vendor in town. The vendor had been cross-eyed. His ophthalmologist, apparently, didn't know his arse from his elbow. But none of that was neither here nor there. What mattered was the here and now. In other words, the present.

And presently, Ricks and Murtow (and the water-buffalo head strapped to Ricks' back) were standing at the bar, trying to catch the attention of the topless barmaid, whose name was a mystery since there wasn't a nametag pinned to her—something topless barmaids everywhere had fought to abolish, and succeeded, just last year.

"Well, isn't this place charming," Murtow said, shaking his head and perusing the joint. "Tash would kick my ass if she knew I was here. I'm going to have to take a shower before I go home. She can smell this kind of thing a mile off."

"I can smell it from here," said Bill, slightly muffled by the poncho concealing him. "Are we in Grimsby?"

"Look, Murtow," Ricks said. "To be a good undercover police officer, we need to do things we wouldn't normally do. You think I *like* being here?" His eyes hungrily followed a dancer as she sauntered past. He licked his lips. "You think I *enjoy* this… this *filth*?" He pouted as a different girl ambled by seductively. "No, but I'm doing it because it's my job. Catching the bad guys. Making them pay for their crimes. Don Paparella owns this place, as well as GANGSTER'S PARADISE, so we need to case the place, gather evidence against Paparella and his boys. *That's* why we're here, Murtow. That's why we're here."

"That was quite a speech," Murtow said. "And I might have believed it if you weren't poking me in the thigh with a massive erection."

Ricks took a step back, but if he was embarrassed by his transgression, he didn't show it.

"There doesn't appear to be any gangster activity going on around here today," Murtow said, searching the bar. "Just a lot of women with their… with their…"

"With their *tits* out, Murtow," said the water-buffalo. "*I* know that and I can't even see them. Speaking of which, is there any chance you guys could cut me some slack, huh? Take the poncho off, Ricks. I'll pretend to be a novelty backpack."

"Too risky," Ricks said. "If it helps, I can describe what I'm seeing to you in vivid detail?"

"That really won't work for me," said Bill. "I'm more of a visual learner, and there are only a few ways you can describe a good pair of boobs without repeating yourself. I'd much rather see them for myself, if it's all the same with you."

Murtow surreptitiously whispered to the poncho and the lump beneath. "You're lucky we brought you along in the first place, bovine. You shouldn't even be here, and by that I mean you're not of this earth. You're dead, should no longer be talking. You're made up of polystyrene and glue. I'd be grateful I could still smell this place if I were you."

"*Is* it Grimsby?" said the water-buffalo.

"How may I help you gentlemen?" said the topless barmaid. She was a handsome lass, if you liked that sort of thing. *She's no Patsy Kensit*, Ricks thought, though she was a steady upgrade from Rene Russo.

Ricks knew how to handle this situation. Girls like this, they wanted only one thing. Respect. Oh, and money, and the occasional bit of dick. Other than that, though, they were—oh, sometimes they liked to be wined and dined, and pretty dresses, they loved pretty dresses, but apart from that, all they wanted was respect. "Nice tits," Ricks said, pointing at the tattoo just above the barmaid's belly-button. "Is that a marsh tit? I recognise the plumage."

The girl brightened somewhat. Running a finger along the tattoo, she said, "Actually, it's a willow tit, and the other one is a great tit." She smiled, primarily at Ricks, which didn't shock Murtow in the slightest since he'd never had much luck with the ladies, had only married one because everyone else in the force seemed to be doing it. "You a fan of tattoos?"

"I'm a fan of tits," Ricks said, nodding his head. "You come here often?"

The barmaid thought about it for a moment. "Every day, really," she said.

"You must really like the place," Ricks said, now in full chat-up mode.

"Not really," said the girl. "Smells like Grimsby."

Ricks laughed, and it was an awful fake laugh, like what you would hear at a Joan Rivers show. "Listen," he said, leaning in closer to the girl, "I was wondering if… what time do you get off?"

"I usually get off in the store-cupboard at around ten, and then after that I work for another few hours, and finish my shift at midnight."

"That's incredibly graphic," Ricks said. "I like that about you… what's your name again?"

"Crystal," said the girl. "Crystal Quim."

"What a wonderful name," Ricks said. "Any relation to Jasper Quim of *The Swan With Three Tits*?"

The girl's eyes filled with panic. "Er, he's my… he's my daddy, but you won't tell him you saw me working here, will you? He'll hit the roof. He thinks I work at a PPI Claims firm."

"We wouldn't dream of telling Quimmy his daughter works in a gangster-owned titty bar, would we, Murtow?" Ricks said.

"I thought we were undercover," Murtow replied. "You can't call me Murtow if we're undercover. That's the whole point of being undercover!"

"Not telling people you're undercover is the whole point of being undercover," said Bill from Ricks' back.

"Who said that?" asked Crystal.

"*I* did," Ricks said. "When I'm not an undercover officer, I like to practice ventriloquism. 'Glue gottles'. See?"

"I saw your lips move," said Crystal.

"That's why I'm practicing," Ricks said. "You don't practice something if you're already good at it. Complete waste of time."

"Well this all seems to be going well," Murtow said with a shake of the head. And inside that head, the words, *I'm too old for this shit*, repeated over and over, like a stuck record or an emergency broadcast.

Suspicious now of the two men standing at the bar, Crystal Quim looked around, perhaps searching for someone to come and save her. It wasn't long before she found what she was looking for. "Paulie!" she yelled. "Might need some help over here."

"There's really no need for any… is that man blind?" Ricks said, mesmerised by Paulie, who was crossing the establishment and bumping into every damn thing in his way. He looked mean, though, whether he could see or not.

"Is there a problem here?" said Paulie Carvalho. "No seriously, is there? I can't see a bloody thing."

Crystal looked from the blind man, to Ricks and Murtow, and back again. "I think these men are undercover police officers," she said, now covering her breasts as if suddenly ashamed of them.

"Oh, really!" Paulie said. "And how do you know they're undercover, Crystal? Did they accidentally give themselves away? Did you see them gesturing to one another in a clandestine manner?"

"They told me," Crystal said.

Murtow kicked Ricks in the shin, and Ricks howled and hopped up and down for a moment until the pain subsided.

"They *told* you they were undercover?" Paulie said. Then, to the empty space between Murtow and Ricks he said, "What kind of undercover cop tells someone they're working undercover, huh?"

"In all fairness," Ricks said, "we've only been doing it for an hour and a bit."

"More to the point," Paulie went on, "what's a couple of undercover police officers doing here at THE PUSSY PALACE, huh? This is a respectable venue. We've had all the greats play here: Cliff Richard – a Tribute, Joe Longthorne, Michael Bubble—"

"It's *Buble*," Ricks said.

"Not *this* guy," Paulie said. "This guy blows huge fucking bubbles. I mean, I couldn't really see how huge they were, but I sure as hell got wet when they popped."

"We're here to see Paparella," said Buffalo Bill. Ricks and Murtow clenched in unison.

"Which one of you pigs fucking said that?" Paulie asked, seething. You could almost see the smoke spewing from his ears. *He* couldn't, of course, but everyone else could.

Ricks and Murtow looked at one another. Ricks wanted to just run, put as much distance between themselves and THE PUSSY PALACE as possible. Murtow wanted to cry, to plead with the blind gangster that this was a very bad mistake, chalk it up as such, and *please don't shoot us in the kneecaps.*

"It was the one with the mullet," Crystal said suddenly. "He's the ventriloquist of the outfit. I didn't see his lips move this time, but that's why practice makes perfect, I guess."

"The one with the mullet, huh?" Paulie said, driving a huge fist into an open palm over and over. "Well, mullet-man, today is going to be a very bad day for you. Don Paparella don't like pigs sniffing around his businesses. Especially undercover ones who are so stupid, they fucking *tell* you they're working undercover."

Just our luck, Ricks thought, *because that's what we are…*

"Now, I'm a nice guy," Paulie said, "so I'm going to leave you both a kneecap——"

"Now would be a good time to run," Buffalo Bill opined, "but of course, what do I know? I'm just a detached head."

Paulie reached into his jacket pocket and pulled out a banana, which he proceeded to point at Ricks and Murtow, but mainly the empty space between them. "Say hello to my little friend!"

"Hello," Buffalo Bill said.

"Erm, that's a banana, Paulie," said Crystal, pointing at the thing in the gangster's hand, more for her own benefit than his.

Paulie seemed taken aback by the revelation. "*Really?*" he said, with some incredulity. "Ah, fuck! My Beretta's in my lunchbox again. Wait here a minute while I…" He turned and began walking across the bar, to where, upon a table, sat a plastic *Wonder Woman* lunchbox.

"We're not really going to wait for him to come back, are we?" Murtow said.

"He's a blind man," said Ricks. "It would be rude to just run away without letting him know first."

"Ricks, he's going to shoot us both in the face," Murtow said through clenched teeth. "Now would probably be a good time to scarper."

"I'm going to have to agree with the sensible black one on this," Crystal said. "You should probably take this opportunity to flee. Oh, and I'd appreciate it if you didn't tell daddy about this, or that I work here."

As Murtow and Ricks hightailed it toward the door, Ricks called back across his shoulder, "You tried to have us killed. Quimmy will know everything by the end of the day." And then they were gone, leaving Paulie Carvalho angry and trying to pull the trigger on a cheese string, and Crystal Quim worried about what her father might say when he discovered his little angel was not quite the angel he believed her to be.

"That's a damn cheese string, Paulie!" Crystal said. "Put it down before you take someone's eye out with it."

16

When DI Tyler woke, he smiled, for it had all been a terrible dream. His eyes closed, he sniggered to himself as he pictured Ethel Gripe sitting there in that rocker. *Ha, how goddamn ridiculous!* And then—in the dream, of course, not in real life, because things like that didn't happen in real life—there was Martin Chuzzlechops, lying on the ground, fighting for breath while those two skunks went at it on top of his head. *Ha, how delightfully surreal!*

"You're thinking it was all dream, da?" said a voice.

Tyler opened his eyes and there, sitting in his lap, was a rat on a unicycle. He screamed, tried to bat the rat away, but he couldn't move. His hands were bound behind his back; he was strapped, rather unceremoniously, to a chair in the middle of the stock room. And there sitting opposite, still performing her Heil Hitler! was Ethel Gripe.

"I think they're going to rape us and kill us," a voice mumbled to Tyler's right. Tyler glanced across and saw Martin Chuzzlechops in the exact same predicament he himself was in: strapped to a chair, smelling of urine, looking terrified beyond belief.

"Actually," said another voice, and Tyler snapped his head across just in time to see the waistcoat-ed fox slowly approach, "one is not in the business of molesting humans. Now, if you were a cat, one would be all over you like a hobo on a ham sandwich."

DI Tyler, panic renewed, struggled to break free of his restraints. "No, this can't be happening!" he gasped. "This isn't real! You're not real!"

"Actually," said the owl watching from the corner of the room, "we are *very* real. We were real before we died, and we are real now." It leapt down from its perch—in this case, a grimy-looking DVD tower—and bumbled toward Tyler, its head swivelling as it went. "And we have a big question for you, copper. You don't mind if I call you 'copper' do you? On account that you are one and 'wanker' just doesn't do you justice."

Tyler might have nodded. It was hard to be certain since he was shaking so much.

"Is this question for both of us, or just the pig?" Martin Chuzzlechops asked. He seemed to have made peace with his maker, and would take whatever the anthropomorphic taxidermy threw at him at this point.

"Just for the pig," said the fox, checking his pocketwatch for the umpteenth time since Tyler opened his eyes. "And might one suggest the truth, the whole truth, and nothing but the truth. You are, are you not, a protector of people, an upholder of the law, and an all-round enemy of bad guys?"

Tyler spat blood onto the Russian rat's head and said, "I'm Detective Inspector Grant Tyler of the Metropolitan Police Force. Of course I'm a protector of the people, an upholder of the law, and enemy of bad guys. That's what they pay me for."

The owl hooted and came to a stop at Tyler's feet, and when Tyler looked down, he realised he was no longer wearing shoes or socks.

"Wha—where are my shoes? What are you going to do to my feet?"

The owl grinned, its head spinning fully around. "What am I going to do to this copper's feet?" it said.

Just then, a baby giraffe emerged from the corner of the room. Sitting upon its back was a two-headed duck. All three of them were grinning maniacally. "Why, I've got a funny feeling in the pit of my stomach," said the giraffe, "that you're about to bite all those toes off if the pig doesn't tell you what you want to know."

"Is that what he's going to do?" said one of the duck heads. "Ew, that's a bit rough. Look at the state of his feet."

"Hooter used to eat baby chicks, for fuck's sake," said the other head. "I'm sure he's not fazed by chowing down on a poorly-manicured foot."

"Please don't eat my foot!" cried DI Tyler, which was a sentence he had never considered using before in his life. Strange how things sneak up on you, isn't it? "I don't know anything! Really, this is all some kind of misunder—"

"'I'm collecting on behalf of Don Paparella' were the words you used when you were riffling through the till," said the owl. "True or false?"

DI Tyler stared down at the owl, incredulous, for a moment unable to speak. What was all this about? Why did they want to know about Don Paparella? Why were these animals FUCKING SPEAKING? All very good questions, especially that last one. Tyler still couldn't believe this was real.

"You might want to answer the owl's question," said Martin Chuzzlechops, head lolling drowsily back and forth and drool stringing from his bottom lip like Spiderman's jizz.

"Shut the fuck up, Chuzzlechops!" Tyler said. "Unless you want to spend the night in the cells."

"Oh, yes, of course," said Martin derisively. "Because

you're in a position to arrest me, strapped to that chair with your shoes and socks off and your willy hanging out."

"My willy is not hanging—"

The unicycling rat rolled from his lap, down his outstretched leg, and onto the ground. And there, as Martin Chuzzlechops had said, was Tyler's willy, hanging out of his flies like a dead witchetty grub. Fortunately, Ant and Dec were nowhere to be seen. "Whathefuck?" slurred Tyler. "My tackle's out! Why's my tackle out?"

"In case I run out of toes," said the owl. "Now, are you going to answer question one, or am I making a start on these… these…" The owl scrutinised Tyler's feet, pecked gently at the emerald toenails. "You know, I'm having second thoughts about this. These are disgusting. I'm usually not squeamish, but these are fucking foul!"

"Eating the copper's toes was *your* idea," said the baby giraffe. "When he was snoozing, you said 'I'll bite his bloody toes off, that'll put the shits up him'. You can't back out now—"

"Okay, *okay*," said the owl. "I just… didn't imagine them to be so filthy, that's all. I said I'll bite his toes off, and I'll bite his toes off. Jeez, talk about peer pressure…"

"I don't know *anything* about Don Paparella!" screeched Tyler. "You don't have to bite anything off." He tried, unsuccessfully, to suck his willy back in through his open flies, but there it remained, looking all forlorn and exposed. "Please, you have to let me go! You're making a big mistake! I'm an honest GAHHHH—"

His scream echoed around the stockroom as the owl's beak clamped down on one of his digits. He continued to howl as the owl—unintentional rhymefoolery aside—ripped through flesh and tendon and bone. Blood sprayed out all over the stockroom floor, pattering down like rain upon the carpet. The pain was immense, like nothing DI Tyler had ever experienced before, and growing up he'd been good friends with a priest. The other dead animals gathered closely round to watch, as close as they could possibly get without becoming blood-drenched participants.

"That's incredible mess," said the rat in broken English. "Who would think so much blood come from just little toe?"

Tyler screamed once more before passing out.

*

Tyler woke to find the monsters still gathered at his feet, only now there was blood—a *lot* of blood—and there, lying on the carpet next to the smug-looking owl, was his severed toe. "Oh, God!" he cried. "Oh, the humanity! How long was I out for?"

"I'd say around seven seconds," said Martin Chuzzlechops. "Long enough to shit your pants, from the smell of it."

Martin was right. Tyler was sitting higher in his seat

now, and there was a terrible smell emanating from beneath him. His entire foot felt as if it had been set on fire, and that was just one toe! He didn't think he could bear to lose any more. "I'll tell you everything you want to know!" he cried at the taxidermy. "Please, just, no more toes. I'm already going to suffer. You've bitten off the little one, see? That's the balancer. I'm going to be toppling over for the rest of my life. Isn't that punishment enough?"

The owl and the fox regarded one another with something like satisfaction. The two-headed duck quacked a couple of times, the Russian rat completed a full-circle of the carpet, leaving a unicycle track in the blood, and the baby giraffe smacked his hooves together in mock applause.

And then the owl leapt up into Tyler's lap and eyed the tiddler it found there suspiciously. "Is this even a willy?" it said. "I mean, I've never seen a human one before, so I don't know, but shouldn't it be—I don't know—less spotty?"

The baby giraffe sighed. "When the copper was asleep, you said, 'I'll chew his dick off! I'll chew his fucking dick off, and I'll regurgitate it, half chewed, and feed it straight into his mouth'. Did you not say that?"

"Do you have to remember every little thing I say?" said the owl. "What, are you making notes, or something."

The baby giraffe held up a notepad. "One of us has to, otherwise nothing would get done around here."

"You did say that," confirmed the fox. "You can't back out now."

"You *can!*" cried DI Tyler. "You can back out whenever you like. The sooner the better, as far as I'm concerned!"

"Shut up, copper!" said one half of the two-headed duck. "You're not getting out of this, so pipe down."

"I did say I'd bite the willy off," said the owl, "but it looks like a bloody aubergine. An aubergine that's gone bad. An aubergine that's been left out of the fridge for all and sundry to take a bite out of."

"Alright," said Tyler. "It's not that bad. I've got an infection at the moment. Try a little tact, yeah?"

"Do you, or do you not, know where we can find the man known as Don Paparella?" said the fox.

Tyler still couldn't believe this was real. It was *Watership Down* all over again, only this time he was going to lose his dick over it. He couldn't rightly tell them where to find the most dangerous fake-gangster in London. If Don Paparella found out he was a nark—and he *would*—then he would most definitely be whacked off. Tyler wasn't an oceanographer, but he knew that 'sleeping with the fishes' wasn't as pleasant as it sounded. "I don't... look, I can't tell you anything because I don't know anything—"

"Bite it off!" mewled the fox.

"Bite that aubergine!" echoed the baby giraffe.

"I don't fancy it!" hooted the owl.

"Out the way!" said the baby giraffe, knocking the

reluctant owl from Tyler's lap, and before Tyler knew what was happening, the creature had clamped down on his manhood. Pain wracked through his entire body. On the seat next to him, Martin Chuzzlechops began to cry. Even Ethel Gripe, who'd remained silent throughout the interrogation, made an involuntary noise.

DI Tyler screamed. "GAHHN!" he said, which meant nothing to anyone. And then he knew he was going to die, and if he was going to die he might as well make the most of it. "*Gangster's Paradise!*" he shrieked as the baby giraffe's teeth clicked together next to his scrotum. "*Paparella's always at Gangster's Paradise! Stop… biting… my dick… off!*"

The baby giraffe took a step back. Tyler saw the penis in its mouth, and now that he saw it in a new light, he realised it *did* resemble an unrefrigerated aubergine. It was uncanny. The giraffe spat it out and began licking its own hooves to remove the taste from its mouth.

"That was incredibly graphic," said the unicycling rat, "and will haunt dreams for years to come."

Blood seeped from Tyler's mouth and geysered from the place which used to house his manhood. This, he thought, was no way for a man to die. He should have gone down in a hail of bullets, like Willem Dafoe in *Platoon*, not losing his penis to a baby giraffe. "I… gergh… dying…"

"One has to agree with you on that," said the fox, checking his pocket-watch. "If one could get a wriggle on, that would be most fantastic. Places to go, people to avenge…"

Tyler took his last breath. If he'd known it was going to be his last, he probably would have made it a deep one, but as he didn't know it was relatively shallow and about as useful as a midget on a basketball team. He slumped back in the chair, occasionally twitching as the life continued to spray out of him.

*

"On a scale of one to ten," Hooter said as he wiped blood from his wing, "one being Disney PG and ten being Takashi Miike, what we just witnessed here was a solid twelve."

On the chair next to the dead DI, Martin Chuzzlechops seemed to realise he was now the only living human in the room, which could only be a bad thing. He began to whistle, hoping the taxidermy didn't notice him.

"Knock that whistling off," said Jemima, waddling toward Martin, who shrank back into the chair in fear.

"Please don't kill me!" he cried. "Please… I don't know what's going on around here, or who this Don Pepperoni is—"

"Shall we go to Gangster's Paradise, guys?" said Gerry, trotting playfully toward the stockroom door.

"Why, that sounds like a marvellous idea," Fairfax said. "One could get used to this murdering malarkey."

"Wait for us!" said Jemima/Jessica, rushing to keep up with the departing animals.

"To the bar!" said Hooter, flying through the open door and out into the shop proper.

"I hope they have vodka," said Vladimir, his tiny wheel squeaking as he pedalled pell-mell after his friends. "And Russian girls. I like Russian girls. Make me homesick. Make me horny…"

There came from the adjacent room a tinkling, as of a bell hanging over a door, and then there was silence. Beautiful silence.

Martin Chuzzlechops finally exhaled. They were gone! The monsters were gone, and they hadn't killed him. They had murdered his missus, and the copper was looking a bit worse for wear, but they hadn't butchered *him!* "I live to fight another day!" he cried. Unfortunately, he didn't take into account the fact he was strapped to a chair in a charity shop stockroom.

Three weeks later, a man by the name of Terry Martin would have the shock of his life while shopping for a new pair of corduroy trousers.

"Bugger," said Martin, for the narrator had said that last part out loud.

17

Ricks' back was starting to ache from carrying the water-buffalo around town, but they were almost there, almost at GANGSTER'S PARADISE, where all the bad guys hung out in one convenient assemblage. It was the perfect place for a final showdown. Ricks could barely contain his excitement.

Murtow was fighting to keep up, breathlessly complaining every so often that he was too old for this shit. "Quit whining," Ricks had told him half a mile back. "At least you're not carrying half a dead animal on your back."

"I'm carrying a hernia on my front," Murtow reminded his partner. "I don't see what the rush is, Ricks. It's not even dark yet. We can't start a final showdown while the sun's still out. It doesn't make for good viewing. The fire won't even show up against the horizon from all the explosions, and if they've got machine-guns we won't be able to make out the tracer rounds."

As much as he hated to admit it, Ricks knew Murtow was right. Sometimes, he was glad his partner was too old for this shit; it meant he was wise, had learned lots of things over the years, like the mechanics of a decent gunfight. Pity they were armed only with truncheons.

"What time's it get dark around here?" Ricks said, slowing his pace.

"What you asking me for?" said Buffalo Bill. "I'm a dead animal head. I don't know shit about shit."

"I wasn't asking you," Ricks said, rolling his eyes. "I was asking my partner."

"Do you know how gay you sound when you say that?" said Bill. "Might as well just pop a dick in your mouth and be done with it."

"All right, pipe down," Ricks said. "Murtow?"

Murtow licked a finger and held it up in the air. Turning this way and that, calculating wind-pressure and whatnot in his head, he said, "It'll be gloomy around seven. It'll be perfectly dark by eight."

"That's a pity," Ricks said, glancing down at his watch. "It's only half-four, and I don't fancy waiting around for three hours for the sun to fuck off just so we can have an aesthetically pleasing final showdown."

"Ricks, are you suggesting we do this right now? In the daylight?" Murtow sounded incredulous. "Are you out of your damn mind?"

"You *know* I am," Ricks said, picking up the pace once again. "I'm the suicidal one with the tragic backstory, and you're the one with the happy family and retirement to look forward to."

"Tragic backstory?" Murtow said. "What tragic backstory?"

Ricks frowned. Surely his partner hadn't forgotten. "You know," he said. "How my wife died, and then I got a dog to replace her, but then that died too, so now I just have a fish?" He tucked his mullet behind his ears. "Murtow, please tell me you remember my tragic backstory."

"I remember you saying something once about how your wife shagged the postman, and then she left you, but I don't remember her dying."

"She's dead to *me!*" Ricks said, suddenly very emotional. "I *trusted* that postman! Even tipped him at Christmas, the conniving little prick!"

"And I don't recall a dog in the story, either," Murtow said. "You don't even *like* dogs, Ricks. You told me you're allergic."

"That's why I'm suicidal, Murtow!" Ricks said. "Can't even pet a fucking shih-tzu without welling up."

"Is that the place?" Murtow said, motioning to a bar at the end of the street. A neon dancer pranced about above its door. The sign said GANG TER'S PARADI E, because recently a neo-nazi had stolen two of the S's for his own personal use. Standing just outside the building, smoking cigarettes and gesturing wildly, were three suited men.

"That's it," said Ricks. "Now remember, we're undercover. We don't *tell* them we're undercover. We keep that part to ourselves and hope they don't notice. If Don Paparella is in there, we get him on his own and ask him to sign the confession. Once he's signed the confession, and I'm sure he will because Italians are usually very honest, we can escort him to the station where he will await trial for mass extortion and the murder of Ted Barker."

"Doesn't sound like much of a final showdown," Murtow said, relieved. "Which is good, because I'm too old for that shit."

"You're forgetting one thing," said the buffalo strapped to Ricks' back. "There are five angry vigilante taxidermy pieces out there, thirsty for blood and vengeance."

Ricks and Murtow exchanged a fearful glance.

"If this is indeed the final showdown, hold on to your hats. It's about to get very messy."

"And on that note," said Ricks. "Let's approach the trio of ne'er-do-wells and gain entry to the bar."

They approached slowly, cautiously, each deciding which Mafiosos they were going to take down should it come to it. Ricks had decided to engage the small one on the right. Unfortunately, so had Murtow. Luckily, it didn't come down to fisticuffs. The three gangsters went back inside just before Ricks and Murtow reached the place.

"Think we scared them off?" Ricks said, rolling his sleeves back down.

"Think they finished their cigarettes," said Murtow, pointing at three discarded, smouldering butts on the ground.

"Are you ready?" Ricks said, taking a deep breath.

"Can we just stand here for a moment?" Murtow said, taking his phone from his pocket. "I want to ring Tash, tell her I love her, you know, just in case things go south in there—"

"Sure!" Ricks said. "I'd ring my wife, of course, but she died in a tragic backstory."

While Murtow waited for his wife to answer the phone, Ricks picked up one of the discarded cigarette butts and began drawing frantically upon it. This was going to be spectacular.

I need a poo, Ricks thought.

Me too, thought Buffalo Bill. *And I don't even have an*

arse.

*

Thumping music spilled from the back door of the club. Michael 'Blue Balls' DeMarco couldn't believe his good fortune as he led the old whore out through the exit and over to the bins.

It was finally going to happen! After all these years, he was finally going to have sex. No longer would he be the laughing stock of the gang. No longer would they cruelly taunt him, or put condoms in his tagliatelle. No longer would he carry the moniker 'Blue Balls'. He would have to change his name to 'Raging Donkey' or something to that effect. He would be able to stand tall and proud, and scream at the top of his lungs, "I had sex with an ugly old prosser!"

"'Ere, less of the ugly, you wanker!" said Cynthia Berk, lighting up a cigarette.

"Did I say that out loud?" Michael was shocked at his behaviour, but it wasn't every day you lost your virginity.

It was today.

And *only* today.

For tomorrow he would be just another man who had had sex. There were millions of them out there, and he was about to join the ranks. He was about to become one of them, and could shout the mantra as loud as he wanted, "I banged a broad in the arse!"

"You bloody well did not and *will* not!" said Cynthia, leaning against the bin with one hand and removing her slightly soiled knickers with the other. "My arse is for

177

one thing and one thing only."

Michael glanced down at the stained knickers in the whore's clenched fist and said, "Yeah, I can see that. Look, less of the chit-chat, okay? I've got to be quick. There's talk of some kind of final showdown, and I really want to be a part of it. If someone's going to get whacked off tonight, I don't want to miss it."

"Money first," said Cynthia, holding out a gnarled hand which looked like a bunch of battered twigs. She wasn't ugly, if witches were your thing, and Michael DeMarco sure wasn't fussy about who popped his cherry. If Camilla Parker-Bowles had shown up in that moment and offered to take over, he would accept. *Filthy*, he was. And horny as hell.

"How much was it again?" Michael said, taking out his *Danger Mouse* wallet.

"Fifty for a blowy with teeth, seventy-five without teeth. A ton for a shag, and a ton-fifty for a shag with no teeth." Her hand remained in place, awaiting payment.

"What if I want to put your teeth up my bum while I shag you?" Michael didn't know whether that was a fetish—this was his first time, remember—but as far as he was concerned it damn well should be.

"I'd rather you didn't," said Cynthia. "So, what's it gonna be, hotshot?"

Michael took out ten twenties and placed them in the whore's filthy palm. "Here's two-hundred," he said, "but I want you to call me Nancy while I do it, and I want you to spit in my eye every now and then, and when I'm close to finishing, I want you to pull my ears and give me your best impression of Ruby Wax."

Cynthia Berk nodded. "Okay, but my Ruby Wax sounds more like Christopher Walken."

"That'll do for me," said Michael, loosening his belt. "In the words of Marvin Gaye, let's get it on."

What followed was the quickest and nastiest sex Cynthia Berk had ever had the misfortune of taking part in, and she'd been a choirboy. Michael 'Blue Balls' DeMarco didn't know his arse from his elbow when it came to intercourse. "That's my elbow you're trying to put it in!" Cynthia had cursed halfway through in her best Ruby Walken voice. Michael had apologised by way of a breathy grunt before trying to locate the mythical vagina, and howling at the top of his lungs, "We're going on an adventure!"

Bent over at the waist like a dusty question mark, the virgin gangster going at her from behind like a dusty question mark jackhammer, Cynthia Berk had wanted to it be over so that she could return to her drink, which had probably been roofied so much by now that it would take a fairy-tale prince—or a defibrillator—to wake her. She would still drink it, of course, because drinks at GANGSTER'S PARADISE weren't cheap, not to mention the fact she quite liked the thought of a week in a coma; it would give her battered kebab time to recover.

"I'm gonna—"

"You're gonna become an astronaut and move to Mars?" Cynthia ventured.

"No. I'm gonna—"

"You're gonna pay me twice as much as we agreed on?" she said, somewhat optimistically.

"No. I'm gonna cuuuuuuuum!" Michael gasped.

"Not in me, you're not!" said Cynthia, lunging forward, breaking their coitus in the process. She was already counting the money Michael had handed her earlier by the time the gangster's orgasm had finished, and what an orgasm it was! There was… stuff everywhere. It was dripping down the walls, down the bin, down the back of Cynthia Berk, down the back of Michael DeMarco—which was a real feat—and down the neon sign hanging over the bar's rear entry. It would take three thunderstorms and a very pissed-off street-cleaner to wash the mess away, but Michael DeMarco had never felt better in his entire life. It was as if a huge weight had been lifted, and in a rather disgusting way it had. He felt lighter… downstairs, could probably cross his legs now if he tried. No wonder people were always banging on about sex; it was the best thing since sliced bread.

"Have you got a piece of sliced bread?" said the whore, pulling her knickers up and wiping semen from her neck with an old newspaper she'd found in the trash.

"Huh?" Michael was still going through those intense few minutes after sex wherein it's difficult to keep one's balance, control one's bodily functions, or manage English words.

"Sliced bread," said Cynthia. "I *always* have a piece of sliced bread after sex."

"Sorry, I… guh…"

"Never mind," said Cynthia, patting the gangster on the back and immediately wishing she hadn't. As she wiped the residue upon the front of her skirt, she said, "Gotta get back to my drink now, lover-boy, but if you're ever in the mood for sloppy seconds, you know where to find me."

"Gungh."

"Gungh indeed," said Cynthia, and she left Michael 'The Stud' DeMarco standing there in the semidarkness with his trousers around his ankles and a dreamy— retarded—smile on his face, and made her way back into the bar.

After exactly eight minutes and thirty-two seconds, Michael 'STD' DeMarco finally had the strength to put himself away. Tonight would be a night he would never forget, and those assholes would have no choice but to believe he had finally popped his cherry, for he had the Chlamydia to prove it and would be suffering its effects for months to come. Still, it was a small price to pay for becoming a man.

Finally.

Slumped against the large bin upon which he had lost his virginity, Michael 'Already Itching' DeMarco lit a cigarette and exhaled a plume of smoke into the cool night air. It was then that he heard a series of tiny voices. Arguing, they were, something about gangsters and the best way to kill them. Michael 'Cockrot' DeMarco pushed off the bin and turned toward the dark area behind it, the place from where the voices seemed to be emanating.

"Hello?" he said, the cigarette dangling nervously from the corner of his mouth. "If you're thinking of killing any gangsters tonight, I'd advise against it. We're all in there. Jimmy the Shit's in there. Vincenzo 'The Snout' Carmichael, he's in there. Hell, Paulie Carvalho's in there, polishing his blind man's cane. You really don't want to do anything silly tonight, whoever you are…" He trailed off there, for the silence which answered him was almost deafening, or perhaps that was just a symptom of his new best friend, the clap.

Someone was there, though. He could make out shapes in the dark. Small shapes. Midgets, perhaps, or girl-scouts. Michael shuddered, for there was nothing worse than late-night cookie-salesmen. "You all need to leave now, before someone whacks you off." As if to demonstrate just how serious he was, he took out a flick-knife, dropped it, picked it back up, fumbled for the blade-release switch, cursed several times, wished the whore was still here to back him up, then finally managed to find the switch which extended the blade.

In the shadows, the shapes moved, whispered conspiratorially amongst themselves. And then came a growl, the likes of which Michael had never heard before, and a fox dressed like something from *Wind in the Willows* sauntered forth, lips drawn back over huge froth-coated teeth.

"What the… fuck… are you?" Michael gasped, suddenly wishing he'd invested in a larger knife.

"Some call me Vulpes Vulpes," said the fox, which was a ridiculous thing for a fox to say. In fact, anything he said—other than an acceptable shriek or a plaintive mewl—was ridiculous. Foxes don't talk, which is why they would make great double-agents. "Others call me 'Gerroffmyland!', but one's real name is Fairfax. One doesn't know what the Latin is for that, but one assumes it sounds remarkably posh."

Michael held the knife out, waved it through the air a few times for good measure, and said, "You… you're not real! You're just some kind of… some kind of post-orgasm hallucination. There's more of *fucks* than of fox about you!"

"Ah, *Dickens!*" said the fox delightedly.

"Who?" said Michael.

"Charles Dickens," said the fox. "One thought… one thought you were altering one of his most famous lines to suit your own purposes, but clearly, from that strange blank look upon one's countenance, one is mistaken."

"I'll cut you!" cried Michael 'Genital Warts' DeMarco. "You come any closer and I'll cut your fucking snout off!"

The fox, seemingly taken aback by his sudden threat, came to a halt beside the receptacle upon which Michael had just lost his virginity. *And it was all going so well*, he thought. *Shot my load, was having quite a good night, and now this! A talking fox adorned in a waistcoat, swinging a pocket-watch and talking in riddles.* It was almost enough to put a dampener on the whole evening. Almost, but not quite.

"Are you familiar with the one they call Don Paparella?" asked the fox, leaning against the slimy bin with one paw. "Looks a bit like Marlon Brando from that film with the horse's head and Adrian out of the Rocky movies?"

Michael didn't know what was more shocking: that the fox knew Don Paparella or that it knew Talia Shire. "Yeah, I know Don Paparella," he told the fox. "What the fuck's it got to do with you, you little ginger bastard?" *I can't believe I'm talking to a fox*, he thought. *I hope it's not like this after every orgasm.*

"Are you familiar with a man named Ted Barker?" The fox drummed razor-sharp fingernails upon the bin. Anyone in the near vicinity would have recognised the opening beat of New Order's 'Blue Monday', but there was no one in the near vicinity.

Michael nodded. "Yeah, that old fucker who liked to fiddle with dead animals," he said, slicing the air with his knife once again for no other reason than to keep up practise.

"Taxidermy," said the fox, "would be a rather different trade if one did not, as you so eloquently put it, fiddle with dead animals."

"I heard he liked to bum them," Michael said. "I

heard he put extra holes in them so he could insert his—"

"You heard wrong," said a new voice, this one from behind him. Michael spun, frantically slashing at thin air with his blade. Sitting upon a set of steel stairs to the right of GANGSTER'S PARADISE was an owl, and when Michael saw it, he knew he had gone batshit insane. "He created us, and your *boss* took his life."

"Your boss, Don Paparella," said a new voice, and out from behind the bin stepped a baby giraffe, "murdered our father in cold blood."

"And for *what?*" said a female voice, and when Michael looked down and saw a two-headed duck staring back up at him, he leapt back in horror, but the duck proceeded even as Michael landed on his ass. "For a couple of lousy British pounds?"

"This is problem," said yet another voice. Michael, lying on the ground and trying not to pass out, snapped his head across to the left to find a rat riding a unicycle ambling toward him. "You are employee of Don Paparella, he who look like Brando in film with sleepy fish—"

"Hey, hey, hey!" Michael gasped, crawling back along the cobbles. "I know the guy. I didn't say I *worked* for him."

"You didn't have to," said the owl, which was now holding something in its talons. A wallet. *His* wallet. The little sonofabitch must have snatched it when he wasn't looking. Fucking owls, man! Can't be trusted. "This card here tells us everything we need to know."

"That's a *library* card," said Michael, now back on his feet and aware that the impossible creatures were closing in all sides, that he was being shepherded as if *he* were the animal.

"Not the library card," said the owl. "This." It held up a credit-card-sized laminated ID, printed upon which were the words Paparella's Protection Services (we eat green berets for breakfast!).

For the longest time Michael was unable to speak, and when he did finally manage something it was garbled and incoherent. "Thasjustatoy!" he said, more than a hint of panic in his voice, for the creatures were almost upon him. By now the fox was licking his lips; it was either going to eat him, or suck him off. Michael didn't know what was worse—passing through the digestive system of an urban menace, mushed up pieces of human and not much else, or being fellated by an urban menace, mushed up pieces of penis and not much else.

"Michael DeMarco," said the owl, and there was a soupcon of finality about the words. "You are hereby sentenced to death for your crimes. You do not have to say anything, but if you have any last words, now would be a good time to use them."

Spinning around, slashing maniacally at the air and the approaching animals, Michael 'AIDS and More' DeMarco said, "Fuck off," and while they were not quite up there with the final words of Jean-Paul Sartre

("I love you very much, my dear beaver") or Kurt Cobain ("Courtney, put the bloody gun down, you'll have someone's eye out!") they were as good as any.

A second later he was buried beneath a mound of writhing fur and feathers, squealing in agony as flesh was pulled from his bones, but thanking the Lord that he was at least going to Hell having had his dick in a lady, or something like one.

18

Reginald Cline, the apparently mad vagabond, had sold everything he had. He had sold his wind-up radio upon which he had followed the exploits of *The Archers* religiously for the past twenty years. He assumed Ambridge would go on existing without his listenership, but where he was going—all padded walls and screaming patients—there was no need to keep up to date with fictional livestock.

He had sold his collection of two-pence coins—five-hundred or so—to the nice man at the corner post office for the fair price of ten-pound-twenty-four. Bedlam was no place for tuppences. Everything was free there; free meals, free bedding, free linen, free daily beat-downs from the psychiatric nurses. Money was unnecessary. Better to drink it all up before he handed himself over to the authorities.

"'Nother pint," he said to the man behind the bar, and he pushed his empty glass in that general direction, knowing that the next time he looked up it would be full.

He had sold his wristwatch to Greasy Mark, a hobo friend of his, for the measly sum of two-pound-twenty, but that was okay since the watch hadn't worked since its battery ran flat in 2011. He had had to wait until 5:14 precisely to make the transaction, however, as that was the time upon which the watch had stopped all those years ago. Greasy Mark was chuffed to bits with his purchase; at least, he had been at the time. Perhaps not so much now that it was almost eight and the watch still read five-fourteen. Still, you get what you pay for, and Greasy Mark deserved a broken watch for being so cheap.

"Two-pound-eighty," said the barman, who looked like he should be an American gangster and yet spoke with all the menace of a Camden cricketer.

Reginald handed the barman a filthy five and went back to staring at his weather-beaten shoes.

Shoes.

There was no need for shoes where he was going. They would make him wear pure-white slippers—no laces, no buckles, just in case he decided to try to top himself—and have him dance around like a ballerina for the entertainment of the wardens. Oh, he knew how it worked, all right. But it was the safest place for him. In there, there would be no talking animals, and that was all a man could hope for in life.

"Here's your change," said the barman. "And might

I suggest that you go get yourself cleaned up in the toilets? If Don Paparella sees you sitting at his bar like that—"

"Like what?"

"Like a hippo's scrotum, he's going to be extremely pissed off, and not just with you, but with me for *serving* you, so why don't you do us both a favour and—"

"Two pints please, and a bowl of water," said a voice, interrupting the barman's reproach. "Hey, if it isn't our friend the beggar."

Reginald's eyes widened, for he now recognised the voice. It was the cops from earlier, the ones with the… monster head… "Nonononono!" he cried, picking up his pint and downing it in one. He climbed down from his stool and, without looking back, ran for the exit, slapping himself occasionally about the face and babbling incoherently about giant demon heads strapped to policeman backs.

*

"I was going to buy him a drink," Ricks said, watching as the homeless man ploughed through the trio of suited business-types standing at the entrance before disappearing out into the night. "Poor fucker."

"You two," said the barman, "smell like cops. Is that what you are? Are you pigs?"

"Can you serve us alcoholic beverages if we are cops?" said Ricks. The barman shook his head and gestured to the door through which they had, only a moment ago, entered through. "In that case, we are construction workers settling in after a long day of bridge-building. This here," —he motioned to Murtow, whose silver eyebrows were knitted together, perplexed— "is Bud McCourt. Bud is a thrice-crowned skittles champion, and yet incredibly humble. My name is Arthur Stoat, and I like girl-on-girl pornography, but not that weird stuff with the balloons and the cats. Puts me right off, that does. We both favour lager, however if you have any suggestions as to what craft ale is available, we are more than willing to listen, but the bowl of water is a must as we are expecting a friend any moment and, unlike me and my heterosexual building partner here, he's very particular."

"Shagging Nuns," said the barman.

"Not recently," said Ricks, frowning. "You would be surprised how difficult it is to find one up for it."

"It's the name of tonight's house ale," said the barman. "And we don't serve bowls of water."

"Well it's a good job we're not bowls of water then, isn't it," Ricks said.

"I'm too old for this shit," Murtow groaned.

"Undercover Cops," said the barman.

"We are not!" Ricks protested. "Did you not just hear our believable backstory? With the girl-on-girl porn and the skittles?"

"Undercover Cops is a light ale we're serving tonight. Piney, biscuity, and yet velvety with low carbonation. Why are you nervously laughing, Mister Stoat?"

Ricks wiped a bead of sweat from his brow.

"Nothing," he sighed. "Nothing, just thought we'd been rumbled, that's all."

"You're an idiot, mullethead," said Buffalo Bill. "Just get the drinks so we can investigate this place more thoroughly."

"Did you say something?" asked the barman. "What's that thing strapped to your back? Are those horns? Are you escorting a horny creature through this establishment?"

Ricks nodded toward Murtow. "He's been married for nearly forty years, so I'd say I guess I am."

"Har-har," said Buffalo Bill. "We're not getting anywhere fast, are we?"

"There it is again," said the barman, now more concerned and peering over Ricks's shoulder in an attempt to get to the bottom of the mystery. "You've got a… a *thing* under there, haven't you? A *talking* thing?"

Ricks cleared his throat. This was not how he had expected the final showdown to kick off. Usually there were bullets whistling through the air, and South African diplomats cursing confusedly. Quite frankly, this was a little underwhelming. "I, erm, that is 'we'," — he motioned to Murtow— "are keen puppeteers, and we are currently working on a new bit featuring a mouthy buffalo head."

"That's right," said Murtow. "As well as construction, skittles, and lesbian porn, we also dabble in ventriloquism."

"That's quite a CV," said the barman dubiously.

"Isn't it," said Ricks. "So if you hear a third voice, it's probably just us working on our new sketch." He was sweating profusely now, like Oscar Pistorius in a line-up. "So how about those drinks?"

The barman sighed. "Utter Bullshit."

"It's the truth!" said Murtow.

"No, Utter Bullshit is an oaky ale with a tangy aftertaste. Two pints, gents?"

Ricks nodded and wiped the sweat from his brow, which glistened beneath the neon lights hanging at the back of the bar. "Two pints of Utter Bullshit it is," he said. "And one for yourself."

The barman set about pouring pints while Ricks and Murtow turned to scour the room, Ricks being careful not to uncover the unearthly creature strapped to his back. "I'm going to have to see," said the buffalo. "If you want me to finger the guy that killed our master, you're going to have to take off this damn tarp."

"If we take it off, do you promise not to draw attention to us?" Ricks began to loosen the straps holding the huge buffalo head in place. Murtow shook his head the entire time, for he was the sensible one of the two and knew a bad idea when he saw it in motion.

"You are puppeteers, remember?" said Bill. "Anyone asks, you can just put your fingers in the back of my head and act like Jeff Dunham."

"This is a bad idea, Ricks," Murtow said. "Why don't we just go. We're not trained for final showdowns.

Leave that kind of thing up to the armed police and the SAS. Besides, I don't know what I've done with my truncheon, and I'm pretty sure I'm touching cloth."

"You're an old man," said Ricks. "A little turtle-head is to be expected." He eased the taxidermy head from his back and lowered it to the sticky bar floor. He folded the tarpaulin back so that the buffalo could see, but didn't uncover it fully for fear it might draw attention to them. They were, after all, undercover.

"Wow," said Bill. "Look at this place. It's like someone watched *The Sopranos*, made some notes, then took those notes to Philippe Starck and said 'Do your worst'." His eyes shifted left and right as he took it all in, scanned the faces of the myriad drinkers. "That guy over there," he said, suddenly.

"Which one?" Ricks straightened up and looked toward the corner.

"The one with thumbs for hands," said Bill. "He was one of them, one of the sonsofbitches that killed Ted."

"That's Marco 'Thumbs' Arminio," said Murtow. "Nasty piece of work, and one of Don Paparella's right-hand-men."

"Is he South African?" Ricks asked.

"What is it with you and South Africans?" said Murtow. "You're obsessed with them. And who the fuck is Patsy Kensit?"

"That's the other one," said Bill, preventing what could have been a quite nasty argument. "He's got teeth of a baby. Very odd to look at."

"Says the disembodied head," said Ricks, focussing in on Rocco 'Baby-Teeth' Gambone, Don Paparella's other right-hand-man. Most people only had one, but not Paparella, the King of Excess. "Okay, so his minions are here, but where's the man of the hour?"

A loud and completely unnecessary throat-clearing turned Ricks and Murtow back to the bar, where the barman stood in front of a pair of Utter Bullshits, one hand out in anticipation of payment. Ricks paid the man and picked up his glass. "We should mingle," he said. "Did you bring the tape recorder like I asked you to?"

Murtow picked up his own Utter Bullshit and nodded. "You really think we'll be able to get a confession out of Paparella? Something tells me he won't be forthcoming with such incriminating evidence."

"We do this my way," Ricks said. "Lots of confusion and gobbledegook, followed by a foot chase through the streets, culminating in a fist-fight on someone's front garden, preferably in the rain while everyone else from the station watches. They will want to break up the fight, but don't let them. It'll be far more dramatic if it's just me and Paparella, all wet and bloody, trading blows and macho witticisms."

"You need help, Ricks," said Murtow.

"I agree with the sensible black man," said the buffalo head. "You're one sandwich short of a picnic, mullethead, and you're going to get us all killed."

Ricks laughed, for he was clearly deranged and should never have been given access to a truncheon, but that was the thing with the British police force: so long as you weren't a career criminal, you could get in. "Don't you two know how final showdowns work?" he said, sipping at his Utter Bullshit and then licking the foam residue from his lips. "It's not all ice-cream and roundabouts, you know. Someone has to get shot in the shoulder at some point, probably Murtow on account of his forthcoming retirement—"

"Why *me*?" Murtow said, exasperated. "I've got a wife and kids. If anyone should be shot in the shoulder it should be you, you fucking lunatic."

"You'll be the hero if you take a bullet to the shoulder," Ricks said. "Your wife will probably fellate you for months to come. Your children will worship the ground you walk on. You'll be the talk of the station, and not just because you took a bullet for me. No. Because you went out with a bang, in style, and you lived to tell the tale, which is a feat in itself given your ethnicity."

"Little bit racist," said Bill from the sticky bar floor. "I'm suddenly rooting for the bad guys, for some reason."

"Look, we're going to make it out of this alive," said Ricks, clinking his glass against his partner's: *chink!*

"Also a bit racist," said Bill. "Tell me, Ricks, are you based on a *Lethal Weapon* character or the real Mel Gibson?"

"I have no idea what you're talking about," said Ricks to the buffalo head. "Let's mingle, and act normal. If these fake Mafiosos figure out we're cops, we're for the chopping block. There ain't much desert around London, but I'm pretty sure they'll have a Joe Pesci type ready to bury us in Hyde Park."

He moved away from the bar. Murtow followed tentatively, suddenly unable to walk normally. As a result, he threw one leg out wide while the other one kept clattering into his own bollocks.

"Wait," said Bill. "You're not just going to leave me down here, are you? What am I supposed to do, huh?" Just then, a twenty-something girl—all breasts and legs and bottom and female body parts—climbed up onto the stool Ricks had just vacated and lit a cigarette. "You know what? Never mind," said Bill, staring surreptitiously up at the girl, who was not wearing knickers; either that or her knickers were made of dark muppet fur. "I'll stay here, make sure things… make sure things don't get out of hand in this…" He trailed off, dreamily appraising the newcomer's undercarriage.

As Ricks and Murtow moved across the room, Utter Bullshits in hand, Murtow said, "Are we seriously going to leave the talking buffalo head over there?"

Ricks shrugged. "It'll be fine," he said, looking back at the preternatural creature. "See?"

Murtow looked, saw the buffalo head's tongue as it lapped at and coiled around a rather seductive-looking lady's ankle. Fortunately, the woman didn't seem to notice, for she was too busy trying to attract the attention of the barman, who was, for some reason or other, trying to make a tea-towel talk without moving his lips.

Just then, there came a tinkling, as if someone was tapping a spoon against a champagne glass in preparation of a big speech, which was, in fact, exactly what it was. Ricks and Murtow turned their attention to the stage at the front of the room, upon which two scantily-clad girls gyrated on poles like epileptic bats, and there stood Jimmy the Shit, glass in hand and suited to the nines. The volume in the room suddenly dropped; a few people continued to mutter and whisper conspiratorially, but they soon shut up when, over in the corner, Vincenzo 'The Snout' Carmichael pulled out a gun and fired two shots into the ceiling. The old lady living in the room above took one to the knee and one to the back passage, but that didn't matter as she had been dead for three months already and her cats—Fluffy, Mittens, and Adolf—had devoured most of her.

"Ladies and Gentlemen," said Jimmy the Shit, "could we have a little silence, please, and a round of applause for the man of the hour. Some of you know him as Brando Lite, while others call him Godfather or Sensei. His name strikes fear into the heart of Cockneys everywhere, and I'm not talking about Boris Johnson." A polite collective giggle and a slight round of applause, just to be on the safe side. "Slowly but surely, brick by brick, he has taken half of this fair city, and we're all going to prosper from it." Cheers and hollers. One of the gyrating strippers fell off her pole and snapped her neck, but it would be an hour or so before anyone noticed. "I give to you all, the gift of… Don Paparella!"

GANGSTER'S PARADISE erupted in a cacophony of rapturous applause and enthusiastic ovations as Don Paparella took to the stage. The place hadn't known a reception like it since Frank Sinatra Jr. ordered an Utter Bullshit.

"Well, this could be easier than we thought," Ricks muttered through the corner of his mouth. "He's going to admit to it right here and now. We'll have him in witness protection by the end of the week. Push record now, Murtow."

"Yeah, about that," said Murtow, somewhat dejected. In his hand he held a 1980s Walkman. You could tell it was a 1980s Walkman because it was wearing a sweatband. "I don't think this thing has a record button."

"That's because it's a Walkman," said Ricks, trying to remain calm. "What happened to the 1980s Dictaphone, the one with the MC Hammer pants on?"

"I must have picked up the wrong thing," said Murtow. "But look. We could always write down everything he says." He took out a pen and a miniature writing pad and flipped to the first blank page. "That's just the same as recording it, isn't it?"

Ricks snatched the notepad from his partner and stuffed it into his pocket. "Shit!" he said. "The final showdown hasn't even started yet and we've already fucked up. Let's just hope those other pieces of taxidermy show up on time to save the day and kill the faux mobsters."

"A little bit far-fetched," said Murtow, "but not beyond the realms of possibility."

Up on the stage, Don Paparella—dressed in the crispest white suit Ricks had ever seen—stepped over the dead stripper and positioned himself in front of the microphone. "Wow!" he said, applauding the applauders for their kind applause. "Just wow!"

In the corner, Vincenzo 'The Snout' Carmichael fired one round into the ceiling—Adolf the fat Siamese didn't know what hit it—and everyone settled down and retook their seats. Only Ricks and Murtow remained standing, for there just weren't enough seats to go round.

"Thanks to Jimmy the Shit for that introduction," Paparella went on, applauding his underling. "How's that IBS treating you, Jimmy?" A big laugh from everyone in the room not suffering from a long-term condition of the digestive system, but Jimmy embarrassedly took his seat, smiling artificially and perhaps hoping the microphone shorted out during Paparella's speech, frying the sonofabitch where he stood. "We are here tonight to celebrate successes. The success of Paparella's Protection Services (Pay up if you know what's good for you!). And the success of Thumbs, who has recently learned to swim. Everyone, please, a round of applause for Thumbs." There followed a round of applause for Thumbs as the odd-handed gangster squirmed nervously in his seat. "We're fortunate to have, performing this evening, worldwide phenomenon, and one of the best tribute acts I've ever had the pleasure of witnessing, The Sammy Davis Jnr Experience." At the back of the stage, behind the crumpled stripper, a small black man waved and grinned. At the front of the stage, Don Paparella lifted a glass. "A toast," he said, "to me. The greatest gangster to have ever owned London apart from those two local lads back in the sixties." As he drank, so did everyone else, and then there was even more applause.

"This is ridiculous," said Murtow. "We're in too deep. These guys are maniacs. They actually believe they're American mafia."

"Who's to say that they're not?" Ricks opined, becoming philosophical for no other reason than the Utter Bullshit had started to work its magic.

"Their parents?" said Murtow. "The fact that they're clearly London born and bred and that they've seen one too many Scorsese movies."

"Who?"

"Martin Scorsese," Murtow said. "*Casino? Goodfellas?*"

"I only know Richard Donner," said Ricks, taking a large gulp of his ale.

"The point is," Murtow press, "that these fuckers are clearly having some sort of mass hysteria. There's no way we should be getting involved in all this. We've only got truncheons."

"That's exactly the kind of thing I'd expect from you, my sensible friend," Ricks said, suddenly feeling a little under the weather. His vision was swimming, and he fought to keep the bile from rising in his throat. "I feel a little… a little…"

"Me too," Murtow said, holding his stomach. "Shit, Ricks, I think we've been spiked."

"How do you know?"

Murtow nodded toward the bar, to where the barman stood, holding a sign with one word scrawled across it in thick, permanent marker, and that word was ZZZZZZ. He seemed very pleased with himself.

"Shit," Ricks said, teetering this way and that, looking for something upon which to momentarily rest his unsteady body, which seemed insistent on screwing him over. "I think they're on to us."

"What makes…" Murtow threw up; and it went on for some time. When he was done, he wiped vomit from his silver beard and straightened back up. "What makes you say that?"

"We have," said the voice from the stage, "some very special guests tonight. All the way from the 1980s, ladies and gentlemen, I give you Ricks and Murtow, a pair of snoopy policemen looking to kick-start some sort of final showdown… or *something*." Don Paparella began to clap feverishly as all eyes turned to Ricks and Murtow, the only men still standing in the room.

"I thought I could smell them!" said a voice, and then

a man stood up, and Ricks and Murtow saw it was the blind gangster they had encountered not too long ago at THE PUSSY PALACE. "Don't believe a word they say! They're not fucking ventriloquists!"

"Ricks, I don't feel too good," Murtow said as he dropped to one knee. "I've lost the use of my legs."

"Plus you're kneeling in your own upchuck," Ricks said, and then he too was forced off his feet. "Don't worry," he said. "This is all part of the plan. We're the good guys in this little narrative. Any minute now something is going to happen and—"

Just then a shrill scream came from over by the bar.

As Ricks went down closing his eyes and clutching his chest, he managed three final words: "Told you so."

19

FIVE MINUTES EARLIER

"Ladies and Gentlemen," said Jimmy the Shit, "could we have a little silence, please, and a round of applause for the man of the hour…"

Buffalo Bill stopped listening after that; he was far too busy trying to cop a peek of the young seductress sitting above him. *I should give her another lick*, he thought, for no other reason than he wanted to, more than anything in the world. She tasted like mint and daffodils, and a little like Grimsby.

He slowly slipped his tongue out once again, and this time he would aim higher. She was like a drug, a terrible, addictive drug; you know they're bad for you—will more than likely see you to an early grave—but you just can't help yourself. And besides, Bill had been dead for a while. The worst she could do was kick him in the face and scream bloody murder. It wouldn't be the first time, and it sure wouldn't be the last.

His tongue was almost up to the woman's thigh when a voice said, "Pssst."

"Well I'll be damned," Bill said as Vladimir tottered back and forth upon his unicycle at the corner of the bar. "If it isn't the Russian rat and his ridiculous ride-on. What's the matter, Vlad? Run out of people to leave hanging on the wall, helpless and unable to move?"

"Don't be like that, Bill," said Vladimir. "We had no choice but to make quick exit. Police were on way, and we're talking animals. Dead, talking animals. What are you doing here? How… how did you arrive here?"

"Got me some new friends," Bill said sulkily, knowing it was a lie. Ricks and Murtow weren't his friends. They had each other; if anything, he was just the annoying sidekick. He'd be fortunate to survive to the end of the final showdown, and he'd most certainly not return in any subsequent chronicles. He was the Sean Bean of taxidermy creatures, and he knew it.

Vladimir looked in the direction Bill was nodding, saw the buddy cop due staring toward the stage, and said, "Those two? Have you lost your mind, Bill?"

"Hey, at least they didn't just leave me hanging there in the shop. You guys abandoned me! I thought we were friends. After all we've been through… and you just… you just…"

A round of applause was followed by a single gunshot. A spot of wee landed on Bill's head; the woman standing at the bar clearly wasn't accustomed to sudden loud noises.

"Holy shit!" said Vladimir, pointing at the stage through the forest of stool legs lining the bar. "That is man who kill master. That is Paparella."

Bill nodded. "That's why we're here," he said. "Pretty sure this is where the final showdown is going to happen. My boys over there are going to bring Don Paparella's empire crashing down—"

"Your boys over there are looking worse for wear," said Vladimir. "How much they drink? Not professional for main protagonists to get bladdered this close to end of story."

Bill shook his head. Ricks and Murtow were swaying back and forth on unsteady legs. Murtow was holding what appeared to be a 1980s Walkman. They looked as if they were having a silent disco, just the two of them. "At least they're doing something about Paparella," Bill said, defending his small, apparently soused army. "Where are the others? Hooter off chasing rabbits, is he? That posh fox having a wank and a cucumber sandwich outside Buckingham Palace?"

Vladimir shook his head. "As matter of fact we are here for final showdown. This is perfect place for suitable denouement." He glanced around at the place, drinking in his surroundings. Then he turned back to Bill, noticing the damp patch just in front of the buffalo head's right horn. "Is that urine on face?" He looked up, saw the undercarriage of the woman sitting at the bar, and held out his tiny hand, testing for rain.

And that was, somewhat fortuitously and more than a little unfortunately, the precise moment the woman chose to look down.

She screamed.

"This not good," said Vladimir as all eyes turned to the hysterical woman at the bar, who was now climbing up onto the stool, trying to put as much distance between herself and the Russian rat on a unicycle as possible.

"It begins," said Bill, and he closed his eyes, for there wasn't much else he could bloody well do.

*

"That's our cue!" Fairfax said. They were backstage, just beyond the curtain which would lead them out onto the stage. Hooter had positioned himself up on the suspended lights, where he could see the entire audience, their faces flashing green and red and blue as the lights changed colours.

"Pull the curtain!" Hooter called, and over to his left at ground level, Gerry grabbed the rope with his teeth and began walking toward the wings. The curtain slowly began to open.

Fairfax, sensing his opportunity, rushed out to centre stage and began to tap-dance. Since he was absent tapshoes, it was all a little pointless, but he enjoyed it nonetheless. But his enjoyment quickly faded as screams and shouts filled the bar.

"Is that a fucking fox?"

"Why's it dressed up like something from *Wind in the Willows*?"

"Why's it dancing like Lionel Blair?"

"Somebody shoot the fucking thing!"

It was the last one which stopped Fairfax in his tracks, and he turned his attention to the man standing at the front of the stage. Don Paparella looked, for some strange reason, amused, as if this was all some kind of game, one which he was winning, one which would only have one outcome. He looked, in other words, like a complete wanker.

"Don Paparella!" Fairfax said, climbing up onto his hind legs and marching across the stage, ignoring the dead stripper at the halfway point. If he'd had sleeves, he would have rolled them up to his elbows. It was that kind of moment. At the sound of Fairfax's voice, the people of the audience gasped in shock. Their mouths fell open in unison, and the temperature in the room climbed so suddenly that Paparella would save upwards of three pence on his next heating bill. "You are hereby charged with the murder of Ted Barker, and mass extortion. One, along with one's friends, is hereby acting as judge, jury, and executioner in this trial. How does one plead?"

The amusement disappeared from Don Paparella's

expression, leaving just anger and bewilderment. "This fucking guy!" he said, motioning the fox. "A proper British fox, threatening me, Don Paparella, the Lord of the City. Ten pounds to the first person to put a bullet in this motherfucker."

People were running for the exits now. Only Paparella's mob remained, and it was a straight race to see which of them could draw their guns first.

A single shot sounded, and the curtain six metres to Fairfax's right billowed out, a smoking hole in the red cloth. "What the…" Fairfax stared out at the dissipating crowd, and standing there, with a cane in one hand and a smoking pistol in the other, was one of Don Paparella's goons.

"Did I get him?" said the goon. "Did I kill the fox?"

Another gangster—this one with a nose which would make Barbara Streisand look like Lord Voldemort—tapped the goon on the shoulder and said, "Of course you didn't get him, Paulie. You're fucking blind. Why do you even have a gun?" To no one in particular he added, "Who thought it was a good idea to give this prick a gun?"

"A little help down here," Fairfax said, for now the final showdown was clearly underway. Shots had already been fired; he was fortunate they had been fired by a man who hadn't seen shapes or colours since 1972.

"Take them out!" screeched Hooter, and he swooped down from the lights, flapping his huge wings and steering himself toward the man standing at the front of the stage, toward Don Paparella, the leader of this ragtag band of fake Mafiosos.

"Kill them all!" quacked Jemima/Jessica, waddling slowly out onto the stage. "Oooh, this one's already dead," she said, stepping over the crippled stripper. "That's lucky."

"I'll take the one with the big nose!" proclaimed Gerry the Giraffe as he trotted down the steps at the edge of the stage.

"I've got blind man," said Vladimir, cycling across the now-deserted dancefloor toward the confused gangster, who was bouncing off things that weren't even there and swinging his cane through the air, hoping to strike it lucky.

"For Ted Barker!" Fairfax yelled. "Vengeance will be ours!"

*

Don Paparella had seen many strange things in his lifetime. As a Londoner born and bred (told you so) he had grown accustomed to the odd and unusual. He had seen men and women painted in shades of grey or gold, pretending to be statues and standing for hours at a time in the middle of the city with just an empty cup and a full bladder for company. He had seen meerkats, recently escaped from the zoo, running through Piccadilly Circus, urinating upon unsuspecting tourists and making a general menace of themselves. He had even seen Napoleon's toothbrush, Darwin's walking stick, and Hasselhoff's swimming costume at an exhibition in Trafalgar; not all in the same room, of course, that would be utterly ridiculous. He had seen all of those things, and yet he had never come across talking animals before.

The owl was upon him, sinking its talons into his shoulder and flapping like buggery. "You little shit!" Paparella gasped, tucking his head into his suit like a frightened turtle. He flailed his arms around, trying to knock the owl away, but the owl was determined, and as it battered him with its huge wings, it said things like, "You murderous sonofabitch!" and, "For Ted Barker! Our master! Our father!"

Ted Barker?

Wasn't that the taxidermist fella? The one he had whacked off just the other day?

"Get the fuck offa me!" Paparella roared, and he sent a fist up toward the owl. It was a soft punch—the kind of punch one might administer to a recalcitrant laptop for fear of breaking it—but he had used his 'ring hand', upon which he wore eight ridiculously large rings. The owl made a noise Paparella had never expected to hear from an owl— "Ooyabastard!" —before flying through the air like a malfunctioning missile and crashing into the bar. Paparella straightened his collar and ran a hand through his hair, slicking it back into place.

"Look out, Vincenzo!" Paparella shouted. A moment later, a baby giraffe thumped into the big-nosed gangster, knocking him from his feet and carrying him back across the dancefloor, where he landed in a suited heap. Paparella wasn't certain, but he thought he could see tiny stars dancing around Vincenzo 'The Snout' Carmichael's head. Tiny stars and a single bluebird.

On the dancefloor, Paulie 'The Blind Man' Carvalho was being circled by what appeared to be a rodent on a tiny one-wheeled bike. *Could this get any weirder*, Paparella thought. And then he thought, *I have to get out of here! They're monsters! Monsters trying to kill me!*

"Thumbs! Baby-Teeth! Come with me!" And with that, he turned and ran for the exit, his hulking lackeys not far behind.

*

Hooter climbed drowsily to his feet, using his open wings to balance. All around him was chaos. Revellers rushed for the exits, screaming and shouting and climbing over one another to escape.

"Is it over?" said a voice Hooter recognised. He turned to find Buffalo Bill pressed up against the bar, eyes closed, shivering ever-so-slightly.

"Bill!" he said. "Good to see you, old friend."

"Hooter?" said Bill, easing one eye slowly open. When he saw the owl he seemed to relax a little. "Hooter! This is crazy. This is—"

"We don't have time for that now," Hooter said. "Did you see which way Paparella and his dirty Ities went?"

"I've had my eyes closed since it all began," said Bill, "but I think they went past me a few seconds ago. I heard the one with thumbs for hands ask for an ice-cream."

Hooter stepped back from the bar, saw the still-swinging Fire Exit door across the room, and adopted the most seriously heroic face he could muster. "I have to go after them," he said. "Wait here." And with that he flew away, leaving Buffalo Bill to contemplate just where else the owl thought he could possibly go.

*

Fairfax chased one of the gangsters backstage; a man by the name of Jimmy the Shit, apparently, for he kept calling back over his shoulder, "Don't you know who I fucking am? I'm Jimmy the Shit! Stop fucking chasing me, fox! I'm Jimmy the Shit! Seriously, fox, you're freaking me out!"

And Jimmy the Shit ran into one of the backstage dressing-rooms and slammed the door shut behind him. Fairfax arrived a second later and, without stopping, barrelled into the dressing-room to find a terrified Sammy Davis Jnr impersonator cowering in the corner, weeping and rocking back and forth.

"Where did he go?" Fairfax whispered to the terrified tribute act. Sammy pointed to a door across the room. Upon the door was a single gold star, and the words, "Tiny Turner' printed in glittery font. Fairfax nodded his appreciation to Sammy and crept up on the door.

They say that foxes are sly, that they are cunning and smart and can outwit most, but the foxes they speak of are alive. As Fairfax carefully approached Tiny Turner's dressing-room door, he stumped his toes twice on the furniture, trod on a piece of Lego, twisted his ankle, and almost swallowed his own tongue. As sly as a fox, it seemed, only applied to those still in the realm of the living, and not those with polystyrene innards.

He eased open the door—which creaked, of course—and heard the quiet sobbing of a lady. When the door was ajar—there was a joke in there somewhere, but Fairfax wasn't in the mood—he saw the gangster, Jimmy the Shit, across the room, one arm wrapped around the tiny neck of a tiny Tina Turner act who was tiny (so tiny was she that she was standing upon her own dressing-table, and still the gangster towered over her). Jimmy the Shit held a nail-file to the poor woman's throat.

"Don't make me do this," said Jimmy the Shit. "I like Tina Turner. She's one of my idols. I'd hate to have to cut the throat of a woman who looks like a miniature version of her."

"Put the nail-file down," Fairfax said, stepping into the room and holding his paws out, placatory.

The gangster looked perplexed. "How can you… why are you talking? You're a fox! Foxes don't talk."

"He's got a point," said the miniature Tina Turner act. "It's a little unnerving, even if you're one of the good guys."

"One is an anthropomorphic fox, replete with human attributes and a darn fine waistcoat, if one does say so oneself." He needed to distract the gangster, and what better way to do that than to bamboozle him with vocabulary. Even as he spoke, Jimmy the Shit's brow furrowed as his brain tried to process the words. The nail-file was slowly inching away from the woman's tiny throat. Fairfax knew it was working. "Did one know that the gestation period for a red fox is somewhere in the region of fifty days? Could one imagine that? Knocked up, and then less than two months later, boom! A litter of cubs."

The gangster's frown deepened. He looked as if someone had just told him the meaning of life, only in Aramaic and without subtitles.

Now is my chance, Fairfax thought, seeing that the nail-file was now safely removed from Tiny Turner's neckline.

He leapt.

Tiny screamed. "We don't need another heeeeeero!"

Jimmy the Shit grunted as Fairfax landed upon his face, wrapping his legs around the gangster's shoulders and bringing his wide-open jaws down onto the top of his head. Teeth penetrated the gangster's scalp, punctured the flesh and sank all the way to the bone. The gangster howled, staggered backwards. Tiny Turner rushed for the door and disappeared through it, screeching, "*I don't wanna fight!*" across her shoulder, because that was the only song title of hers which made any sense in that moment.

"Gngh!" said Jimmy as he slumped to the floor, his eyes flicking around the room as if trying to process where he was and what was happening.

Fairfax bit deeper. There was an audible crunch—

like someone noisily eating cereal or a child's foot being run over by a steamroller—as his teeth breached the gangster's skull, and pretty soon after that, Jimmy the Shit stopped struggling. His final words were, "Rainbow buttercup cheese and Kanye", for the brain is a very fragile thing. Like a tin of tuna or a roll of camera film, once exposed, it's not much good for anything other than the bin.

Jimmy the Shit twitched involuntarily as blood dripped down his face and his eyes glazed over. He was dead. Deader than Bill Cosby's career. And Fairfax felt good for killing him.

"Serves one right," said the fox, as he climbed off the gangster and gave his waistcoat a once-over, just to make sure none of the blood had spattered him. Satisfied that he wouldn't have to make an impromptu visit to the dry-cleaners, Fairfax ran for the door, past the still-cowering Sammy Davis Jr act, and headed for the stage.

*

Vincenzo 'The Snout' Carmichael had never wrestled a baby giraffe before, which was probably why he wasn't very good at it. From what he could tell, it was all about limbs. Limbs and necks. The baby giraffe favoured its neck as a weapon, swinging it violently through the air, clattering its immature ossicones against Vincenzo's own head and chest. It hurt like hell, but Vincenzo wasn't going down without a fight. He was, however, going down without a gun, for the one he had had just a moment ago had been unceremoniously purloined and lobbed across the room by the irate mammal, who clearly wanted this to be a fair fight, or something like one.

"Shouldn't you be in a zoo?" Vincenzo grunted as the baby giraffe swung its neck once again in his general direction. Vincenzo leapt back, dodged the creature's rapidly-shifting head, and retaliated with a quick one-two jab. The giraffe's head snapped left and then right in ultra-slow-mo, drool flying through the air as its mouth flapped open and shut and its invisible gum-shield disappeared down the back of its throat.

"Shouldn't *you*?" said the baby giraffe, recovering quickly. "Your nose looks like… like something that should be seen in a zoo." It wasn't the best comeback ever, but what did you expect from a baby giraffe. He dropped the nut on the gangster and then hoofed him twice in the bollocks for good measure. Vincenzo squeaked, for it doesn't matter if you're a made wiseguy or not, a pair of swift knocks to the Jacobs will have you singing like Justin Bieber after an all-you-can-eat helium party.

Vincenzo went down clutching his nethers and sucking in lungfuls of air which wouldn't make a blind bit of difference. "You… what *are* you?" He knew it was a giraffe, a young one, but that wasn't all it was. It was a talking giraffe. And talking giraffes, Vincenzo knew, were the thing of fairy-tales. Aesop, that well-known ancient Greek fabulist—not to be confused with the *other* Aesop: Association of European Schools of Planning—had a lot to answer for.

The baby giraffe stood over him looking down. The nightclub lights flashed green and blue and red upon its red and brown polygonal patches, giving the creature a somewhat psychedelic mien. "I'm your worst nightmare."

"Actually my worst nightmare is being caught riffling through my mother's knicker drawer while rubbing myself ferociously and singing God Save the Queen."

"Then I'm your *second* worst nightmare," said the giraffe.

"That's more like it," said Vincenzo, and then the baby giraffe's hooves rained down upon his face over and over and over again. His huge nose broke and then came away completely, leaving just a pair of holes in its wake. Flesh ribboned and fell from his head in clumps, and he howled and tried to scramble back, away from the demonic giraffe and its dance of death, but to no avail.

A second later, Vincenzo 'The Snout' Carmichael was unconscious.

And ten seconds after that, his face had been flattened so much, you could have put it in a frying pan, drizzled it with lemon, and tossed it.

*

Fairfax arrived back in the main room just in time to see Gerry the Giraffe's sick Riverdance. Of Don Paparella there was no sign, and his lackeys were missing, too. *Oh no!* Fairfax thought. *They've escaped. This is all for nothing!*

"Little help over here!" said a voice from the dancefloor. Fairfax spun, saw Vladimir unicycling around the blind gangster—who was swinging his cane through the air optimistically, hoping to strike his tormentor—and rushed to his aid.

"Have you seen Hooter?" Fairfax asked Vladimir, ducking beneath the cane as it whipped through the air.

"If haven't notice," said Vladimir, "been busy keeping crazy blind man at bay." He was pedalling pell-mell, his tiny legs moving somewhere in the region of 120rpm. "We should have planned better," he said, breathlessly. "I have no weapon. This bad organisation. Blind man have stick."

"Leave it to me," said Fairfax. How hard could it be to kill a blind man? He was just about to lunge at the gangster's throat, tear it completely out, when Jemima/Jessica dragged themselves across the dance-floor, spilling stuffing and feathers everywhere and leaving a bloody snail-trail in their wake. They were barely held together now; a perfect cut had almost sliced them apart right down the middle. "What happened to you two? Which one of these assholes did it? Where's that blood coming from?"

"Actually," Jemima said, "we were in the middle of a fight when we decided to split up."

"Didn't really think it through," Jessica said. "And the blood's not ours. We're as dry as a bone, but we thought it would be more dramatic if we smeared it all over us.

Is it working?"

Just then, the blind gangster's cane whooshed through the air, connected with Vladimir, and sent him—and his unicycle—hurtling toward the dead stripper on the stage. As he went he yelled, "From Russia with looooooove!", which was a strange thing to say at the best of times.

Fairfax turned and snarled at the blind man.

"Oh, you want some?" said the man, whipping his cane through the air willy-nilly. "I'm trained in the ancient art of blind Kung-Fu. I can smell my enemies, know when they're going to attack, feel when—"

Fairfax kicked the blind gangster in the face. As the gangster landed with a thump on his back, the fox whipped out his pocket-watch and began swinging it wildly around his head and body. "Whoooooaaarrr!" he said, controlling his pocket-watch with no small amount of expertise. "Whooaaarrr!"

Jemima/Jessica dragged itself over to the felled gangster and began pecking at his eyes. *Dink, dink, dink!* After a few seconds they realised it was pointless. Jemima, from somewhere or other, pulled out a cutthroat razor and ran it along the blind gangster's throat. Blood geysered out as the gangster choked and wildly thrashed, clutching at his freshly-slit throat as if it would make a blind (pun intended) bit of difference.

"That was incredibly graphic," said Fairfax, pocketing his pocket-watch. "One has never seen such... such bloodthirsty abandon, and one went to

Eton."

The blind gangster, after almost a minute of wet choking sounds, fell still. Blood continued to pump from the slit in his throat, but it had become laboured, as if his heart had decided it really wasn't worth the struggle. He was dead. Deader than Rolf Harris's painting career.

To the two-headed duck Fairfax said, "Did either of you see which way Hooter went?"

"He went after Don Paparella," said Jessica. "That way." As she lifted her wing, it fell off completely. "*Fuckit!*"

"Nothing a bit of glue won't fix," said Fairfax, running toward the exit.

"Hang on!" quacked Jemima. "Where are you going?"

Fairfax, without turning or stopping, said, "One is going to avenge our master." *And save that damn reckless owl in the process*, he thought but didn't say.

*

Cynthia Berk woke up to numb legs, for she had fallen asleep on the toilet yet again. Luckily, this time she was facing the right way. She gave herself a perfunctory wipe— "Have I even pooped?" —stood and pulled up her drawers.

She left the cubicle, yawning, and made her way across to the large mirror, where she gave herself a once-over, saw that there was only so much you could polish a turd, and decided not to bother reapplying her make-up, most of which she now wore on her knees.

Once all feeling returned to her legs, she made her way toward the door and the club beyond. Hopefully it hadn't missed her.

She pulled the door open, saw the carnage, saw the dead gangsters scattered about the place and the baby giraffe busting shapes on the dancefloor, saw the two-headed duck seemingly operating upon itself with a cutthroat razor, saw the unicycling rat feeling up a dead stripper, saw the buffalo head nestled beneath the bar with its eyes shut tight and its lips moving as if in silent prayer, saw *all* of that…

And then passed out.

*

The car below—an expensive-looking thing with chrome wheels and a private number-plate which read PAP 1—swerved dangerously across the road, veering left and right to avoid those drivers adhering to the speed limit. Hooter, fifty feet above the racing vehicle, had probably the best view in the house, the kind of view one only got when a TV station helicopter's pilot was feeling particularly daring during a pursuit. It was all Hooter could do to keep up. He was flapping like a madman, swooping down every now and then to avoid telephone wires or electricity cables. The fact of the matter was, Hooter hadn't flown for a long, long time, not since that fateful day in which he'd regrettably picked a fight with a double-glazed window. He had forgotten how hard it was.

Breathing heavily, Hooter kept pace with the vehicle as best he could.

Paparella could not, he thought, be allowed to escape.

*

"Is it still up there!?" Don Paparella said, avoiding a milk-float which had no right being out at this time of night. He honked his horn thrice as he passed to let the driver of the float know what an absolute dickhead he was.

"I can't see it!" Thumbs yelled. He was hanging half out the passenger window, looking up for the owl which had been tailing them ever since they'd left GANGSTER'S PARADISE. "Oh, hang on. There it is! It's still up there, Don! What are we going to do?"

"We're going to die!" Rocco 'Baby Teeth' Gambone screeched from the back seat. "It's not going to stop until we're dead!"

Don Paparella hammered the steering wheel twice with his palms. "Shit! Fuck! Shitfuck!" He composed himself, taking several deep breaths and a handful of Calms (other homeopathic nervous tension relief tablets are available) before speaking again. "It's just an owl, for Christ's sake. I'm not afraid of a fucking owl."

"I hear they're possessed by ancient African demons," said Thumbs, winding his window up and shuddering like a shitting dog. "That's why their heads turn all the way around."

"I've heard they have three sets of eyelids," said Baby Teeth, nervously. "One to sleep, one to blink, and the third to stab you in the face when you're not looking."

"Will you two get a grip!" Paparella said, avoiding a truck laden with precariously-arranged logs, for he had seen the *Final Destination* movies and wasn't a complete idiot. "It's just an owl. An ordinary owl."

"It talks," said Thumbs. "Ordinary owls don't talk."

Okay, Don Paparella thought, *that is a little strange*. But parrots talked, and ravens were known to converse from time to time. Foxes, on the other hand, that was a first for him, and two-headed ducks, granted, had no right to be walking around let alone speaking the Queen's English.

Paparella, approaching a slip-road, dragged the wheel hard to the right, steering the Mercedes down toward an A-road. "Can someone check to see where the fucking owl is?"

Thumbs reluctantly wound his window down and stuck his head through it, which was the right order to do it. "It's still up there," he said. "It's giving me the finger."

"Shit!" Paparella said, hitting the wheel again, this time with his fist. He glanced into his rear-view mirror, for there was a single light there, a solitary beam approaching just beyond Baby Teeth's stupid round head. "We've got company," he said.

Baby Teeth spun in his seat and glanced through the rear window. "Is it the cops?" he said.

"We half-own the cops," Paparella said, hoping that, if it was the police, it was the half they owned and not one of the good guys. "But I don't think it's them."

Baby Teeth wound down his window and peered out. As he watched the vehicle approaching from the rear, his huge ears flapped about in the wind. "You're never going to believe this, boss!" he said.

Don Paparella cursed. "What now?"

"There's a fox out here on a motorbike."

Of course there is, Paparella thought, shaking his head. *Of course there fucking is.*

*

Fairfax had never felt so cool. It was true what they said: four wheels move the body; two wheels move the soul. Fairfax's soul was somewhere back on the pavement outside GANGSTER'S PARADISE, where he had gone hand-to-hand with a Hell's Angel and, thanks to the guy's gimpy leg and severe drunkenness, had won. Thusly, he was now the proud owner of a Harley Fat Boy, and he was gaining on the Mercedes, could make out the flapping ears of the head sticking out of it.

Overhead, Hooter swooped through the night. *He probably has the best view in the house*, Fairfax thought. *The kind of view one only gets when a TV station helicopter's pilot is feeling particularly daring during a pursuit.*

Just then, the Mercedes switched lanes, and Fairfax saw the barrel of a gun protruding from the passenger-side window. There was a muzzle-flash and a loud bang. Fairfax pulled the huge bike to the right, his furry knee brushing the tarmac as it went. For a moment, he thought he was going down, that there was no way he could control such a big bike and that he'd been a fool to take it in the first place, but then it popped back up and he was straight again. Straight, and not leaking stuffing, which was a miracle.

"Who do you think you are shooting at, you dastardly rogues!" Fairfax said, twisting the throttle and pulling up alongside the Mercedes on the driver's side. Don Paparella glanced out, his eyes wide and his mouth agape. Anyone would think he had never seen a taxidermy fox riding a Harley Fat Boy before.

Fairfax drew one paw across his throat—the universal sign for 'You are fucking dead when I catch you!'—and dropped back behind the car just in time as Paparella steered hard to the right in an attempt to topple the bike and its rider. The front wheel of the bike grazed the Mercedes' bumper, and Fairfax dropped back another few feet, somehow managing to stay upright.

In the sky above, Hooter hooted.

"Yeah, yeah, Hedwig," said Fairfax. "You couldn't even reach the accelerator, you fluffy rascal."

*

"This is getting ridiculous!" Paparella said, flooring the accelerator. "It's like a *Pulp Fiction* version of *The Animals of Farthing Wood*."

"That would probably make a great tagline," said Thumbs as he fed bullets into a fresh magazine. "If this were a book or a movie," he added.

"Well it's not!" said Paparella. "It's real life, and we're

fucking in it!" A quick glance at the rear-view mirror told him everything he needed to know: the fox was still on their tail. "Are you nearly done loading that thing?"

Thumbs held up his hands. "I find it hard due to my lack of motor skills and general coordination brought on by the fact that I only have thumbs for hands."

"Give the gun to Baby Teeth," grunted Paparella.

"But Baby Teeth's a terrible shot—"

"You've got thumbs for hands!" Paparella shouted angrily. "Give Baby Teeth the gun now or, so help me God, I'll ground you for a fortnight."

Thumbs reluctantly passed the gun to Baby Teeth, who seemed pleased with the transaction. "Pew! Pew! Pew!" he said excitedly. Then he sang, "I've got the guuu-uuun, I've got the guuu-uuun, I've got the—"

"Shoot the damn fox with it!" Paparella said. "Quick, he's coming up on your side."

Baby Teeth leaned out of the window—in hindsight he should have wound it down first—and once the glass stopped tinkling to the road rushing by underneath them, he levelled the gun at the fox and pulled the trigger.

*

Fairfax didn't feel the bullet rip through his shoulder, but there was an explosion of polystyrene. "Gosh," he said. "One is hit." He glanced toward the Mercedes, saw the grinning face and the gun sticking out of the rear window, and dodged a second bullet by mere centimetres. In fact, so close was it that he heard it whistle by, felt the wind as it sped past. A couple more inches and it would have ripped his nose clean off.

This was getting dangerous.

In the night sky above, Hooter hooted.

"Oh do shut up!" Fairfax angrily said. "Why don't you come down here, if you think you can do any better."

*

Up ahead, a bridge loomed on the horizon. Lights stretched from one side to the other, and cars languidly ambled across it, unaware of the high-speed pursuit taking place just a few hundred yards away.

One man who saw the Mercedes coming was Reginald Cline, the crazy hobo, who was sitting on the bridge, legs dangling over the edge, awaiting the right time to drop down and put an end to his misery. He didn't want to spend the rest of his life in an institute, being buggered by the orderlies and spoon-fed carrot soup three times a day. That was no way to live, and so he had decided to end it all, to go out with a bang—and probably a crunch, and maybe a squelch, but hopefully he wouldn't hear that.

This is it, thought Reginald. The car barrelling toward him on the road below was doing a fair speed, enough to finish him off if the sixty-foot drop didn't. He shuffled his bottom closer to the edge, ignoring the horns honking as the cars passed by on the bridge behind him.

"Do it, you bum!" said one voice.

"Yeah, do it, you fucking tramp!" called another.

People weren't as friendly as they used to be. Reginald Cline wouldn't miss the world, for it had gone to Hell in a handbasket.

He waited for the right time.

The Mercedes drew closer.

And he waited.

And then he saw the owl tearing through the sky, about to slam into his face, and he fell off the bridge in what could only be described as a terrible anti-climax.

*

"Look out!" Thumbs cried as the lights of the Mercedes fell upon a splattered body, just lying there in the middle of the road. How inconvenient.

Don Paparella slammed on the brakes and the Mercedes screeched as its wheels locked, and yet it still ploughed implacably on toward the exploded corpse beneath the flyover. The smell of burning rubber suddenly filled the car. In the back seat, Baby Teeth started to cry, for he had dropped the gun out the window and he knew how much trouble he was going to be in should they survive the next five seconds. In the passenger seat, Thumbs assumed the position— head between knees, arms on head, legs crossed to prevent the wee from coming out—and began to pray.

And still the car screeched.

Don Paparella's entire life flashed before his eyes. There he was suckling upon his mother's breast; and there he was graduating from school with a 2:1 in Art and Design; and there he was changing his name by Deed Poll from Kevin Stewart to Don Paparella. Unfortunately, that was as far as he got before the car stopped suddenly and momentum carried him forward, out of his chair and out through the windscreen, for he had forgotten to put on his seat-belt, the daft git.

The windscreen exploded outward as three men—two of them larger than the aperture—came through it. At least one of them was still crying.

*

Climbing down off the motorcycle, Fairfax followed the trail of blood and shredded skin along the road. It was like Hansel and Gretel, if only Hansel and Gretel had been directed by Takashi Miike, and instead of breadcrumbs the trail comprised of teeth and chunks of flesh. Some of the teeth were tiny, too, which was very strange indeed.

Fairfax followed the blood and viscera—it was a very nasty accident—for almost twenty feet, eventually arriving at the bodies.

"Gosh!" said Fairfax, for what he saw was certainly worthy of such profanities.

Three bodies lay mangled, bloody limbs intertwined as if in the throes of some gory homosexual orgy. "Ooh, an anagram," said Fairfax, rather pleased with himself.

Just then, the bodies began to move, and from somewhere deep beneath the carpet of arms and legs came an almighty groan. Fairfax stopped; he hadn't planned on battling the undead tonight—had left his zombie-killing gear at home—so he figured it best to remain at a safe distance.

But Paparella wasn't rising from the dead. He wasn't quite dead, you see. He pushed himself up, peeled his lackeys' body parts from him with an expression of disgust, and levelled the gun in his hand at Fairfax.

"Well this is surprising," said Fairfax, surprised.

"Not really," said Don Paparella, shaking. He reached into his mouth and pulled out a loose tooth, which he flicked toward Fairfax. "This is the final showdown. It wouldn't be a good one if there weren't one or two false deaths. Keeps people on the edge of their seats."

Fairfax looked at the gun, looked at the man holding it, and knew he was in a bit of a pickle. He wasn't sure if he could die—since he was already dead—but he imagined that, if he lost enough stuffing, it wouldn't be a good thing. "Would one put the gun down?" he said, optimistically.

"Not on your nelly," said Paparella. "This is only going to end one way, and it's not looking good for you, gingerbollocks." He thumbed back the hammer—*click*—and smiled a bloody smile. "Goodbye, fox who talks…"

All of a sudden, as things are wont to happen in such situations at the end of a particularly long and arduous plotline, there came a shrill hoot, and then a blurry shape whipped through the air between Fairfax and the gangster. The gun, a millisecond from firing, was no longer in Paparella's hand, and so Paparella was left pulling an invisible trigger, confusedly. After a few seconds he noticed that the gun was gone, and said, "Where's my gun gone?" just to demonstrate the fact.

Fairfax smiled knowingly as a flutter of wings to his right parted his fur and fairly gave him a shiver. "You'll have to do the honours," said Hooter, now landed beside the fox and holding the gun out for him to take. "Don't have opposable thumbs."

"Neither do I," said Fairfax, accepting the gun. "But if one can ride a Harley Fat Boy, one can darn well pull a trigger." He raised the gun, training it upon Don Paparella standing over the mutilated bodies of his former subordinates.

"You don't have to do this," Paparella said, nervously. "I'm not a real gangster. My name's Kevin. In my spare time I like to draw fruit-bowls—"

"You killed Ted Barker," said Fairfax, cracking his neck and staring along the short length of the gun. "He was our creator, our maker, our father, and you murdered him in cold blood."

"—and I have two goldfish I need to feed. You kill me, you're not just killing me; you're killing Chas and Dave—"

Fairfax pulled the trigger.

20
The End Bit (Where Everything Gets Tied Up Nicely in a Little Bow)

Standing at the edge of the forest, Fairfax and Hooter felt as if they had been given a new lease of life. Contained within these trees was everything they needed to survive; a second chance at life. It had taken them almost three days to reach the start of Epping Forest, and now that they stood before its wondrous possibilities, they both saw that it was worth it.

"Well, I guess this is it," said Hooter.

"One guesses so," replied Fairfax, stripping out of his waistcoat and placing it on the ground. When Hooter was about to ask him what he was doing, he said, "There's no point dressing like nobility if one is to return to one's roots." He took one final glance at his pocket-watch, and placed that on top of the discarded waistcoat. "And besides, one does not need stylish clothes to define one's personality."

Hooter's beak curled into a little smile. "So what are you going to do now?" he asked. "Find a pack? Settle down? Have some cubs?"

"You do realise that we're still ninety-percent stuffing, don't you?" Fairfax motioned to his own body.

Nodding, Hooter said, "Yes, but we are more alive now than we ever were before." Whatever the hell that meant.

"What about you?" Fairfax said. "Just going to fly

around, hooting? Making your head spin around for no good reason other than it looks scary?"

"That's the plan," said Hooter. "I might pop out of the forest every now and then to shit on an immigrant's car, but yeah, flying, hooting, spinning is going to take up the majority of my time."

"Sounds good."

"It does. It really does."

"Well, I guess this is it," said Fairfax.

"We've done this bit already—"

"Yeah, let's just get it over with—"

"Deal."

They walked toward Epping Forest, the fox and the owl, having just lived through a fable Aesop, in his wildest dreams, could never have concocted. Nor would he have wanted to.

*

"Come on, Mommy," said Cindy Koontz, rushing toward the pond at the bottom of the hill, a half loaf of bread dangling in its bag from her tiny child-hand. "I can see the ducks, Mommy! I can see them, and they look hungry!"

"Slow down, sweetie," said Cindy's mother. "You're going to fall." *And skin your knee, you little shit. Plasters aren't cheap, and I'll have you whining all fucking night about how sore you are.*

"Look at the ducks, Mommy!" Cindy said, excitedly, coming to a halt next to the pond.

"I know, sweetie," said Cindy's mother, still twenty

feet away. *I've seen ducks before, you little twat. They're shit. Quack, fucking, quack. Why don't you just jump in the pond and live with them, you love them so much.* "Be careful, sweetie. Not so close to the edge."

Cindy began tearing pieces of bread and launching them as far as she could. Ducks began swimming across the pond toward her, keen to get their fill of bread, despite recent warnings that it wasn't good for them at all, and that anyone who fed them bread was an asshole, even this cute little girl.

Asshole.

"Don't feed all the same ones," said Cindy's mother. "You don't want to make them fat." *Throw the bread further, you little… you know what? Do whatever you like, spoilt git. I hope you get meningitis—*

"Look, Mommy!" said Cindy. "Those two are just half-ducks." She screamed as if she's seen a ghost or Jimmy Saville.

"Don't be silly, Cindy," said her mother. "Half-ducks don't exist." But then she saw, out on the pond, a pair of half-ducks, swimming around in perfect circles as if confused. And she screamed too.

If she and her daughter were closer, they would have been able to hear the ducks talking to one another.

"We really didn't think this through," said one.

"We really didn't," said the other.

*

Gerry the Giraffe rocked back and forth, back and forth, the little boy riding him playfully yee-hawing like a little cowboy.

There are worse ways this could have gone, thought Gerry. And then, as the boy smacked him on the back of the neck and climbed down, leaving Gerry swaying slowly on the wooden rockers unceremoniously nailed to the bottoms of his hooves, he said, "Fuck my life."

*

"Ladies and Gentlemen," said the ringmaster of WILD MAC'S CIRCUS (Bendy people are our specialty), "Our next act comes all the way from Moscow, drinks Vodka like a legend, and despises President Putin as much as the next man." The audience—a full-house—cheered and applauded, for they knew what was about to happen, had driven halfway across the country just to see it. "He's three-inches tall without the wheel, but don't let that put you off. It is our pleasure to announce the final act of the night… give it up for Vladimir the Unicycling Rat!"

Rapturous applause almost brought the tent down as out onto the stage rode Vladimir, a bottle of Smirnoff in one hand and three juggling balls in the other.

"Vlad! Vlad! Vlad!" the audience chanted.

There are worse ways this could have gone, Vladimir thought, for he'd seen what had happened to Gerry the Giraffe and didn't envy the poor fucker one bit.

*

"Freeze!" said Murtow as he and Ricks forced their way into the drug-den. Upon tables, white powder lay scattered. Bags of cocaine were stacked neatly on pallets all around the room. The three men at the centre of the room—Carlos, Marco, and Luiz Rojos—reached for their machine-guns, but stopped suddenly when a deep voice said:

"I wouldn't do that, if I were you."

"What the hell is that?" said Carlos.

"It looks like a buffalo head on a stick with a rifle strapped to its horns!" said Marco.

"That's *exactly* what it is," said Ricks. "You have the right to remain silent. Anything you do say will be taken down…"

*

At the edge of Epping Forest, all was quiet. Night had fallen, the moon was high in the sky and, beyond the clouds, stars had started to emerge. The waistcoat and pocket-watch, undisturbed since earlier that day, were suddenly snatched up by a ginger arm. Fairfax, that cunning, wily, posh-as-hell fox, pulled himself into the waistcoat and tucked the pocket-watch away before running back into the trees. To hell with nudity, thought the fox as he went, for it got cold in the forest at night.

In the treetops, an owl hooted.

"Whatever, Hooter," grumbled Fairfax. "One step at a time, yeah?"

THE END

P.S. No animals were harmed in the writing of this book. However, it was printed on what used to be a squirrel's bedroom. Sorry.

www.adam-millard.com